DARK OATH

A DARK SAINTS MC NOVEL

JAYNE BLUE

NOKAY PRESS LLC

Copyright © 2018 by Jayne Blue/Nokay Press LLC

All rights reserved.

No part of this book may be reproduced in any form or by any electronic or mechanical means, including information storage and retrieval systems, without written permission from the author, except for the use of brief quotations in a book review.

This is a work of fiction. Names, characters, businesses, places, events, and incidents are either the products of the author's imagination or used in a fictitious manner. Any resemblance to actual persons, living or dead, or actual events is purely coincidental.

DON'T MISS A THING!

For exclusive news, sign up for my Jayne Blue's Newsletter. You'll get a FREE BOOK as a welcome gift!

Chapter 1

DEACON

BLESS ME FATHER, for I have sinned ...

Incense filled my head, my senses, making me sway for a moment as the hardwood of the kneeler cut into my kneecaps. Canned harp music softly played from speakers hidden behind two fake ferns on either side of the wooden podium at the front of the chapel. A wooden cross hung on two wires behind it. To complete the effect, they'd hung two identical fake stained-glass panels on either side of the room. Instead of depicting a saint or a station of the cross, the panels showed a nurse in an old-fashioned white uniform ministering to a wounded man who smiled up at her.

This wasn't my church. Still, the incense pricked my sense memory enough that I could close my eyes and find myself right back there, laying out Father Sanchez's vestments as he quietly sang. I found peace in the memory. Father would quote scripture as he stood, bent-backed as I helped him straighten his collar.

"Time to go to work, son," he would say, his eyes crinkling with joy. Then he would take a deep, heaving breath and turn toward the door.

"Son?"

My eyes snapped open. The odor of strong antiseptic and sickness joined the incense. Behind me, a P.A. blared an electronic bell, paging a code team to the maternity floor. I made the sign of the cross and said a quick prayer that they moved swiftly.

"Son?"

His voice hadn't changed. Very little about him had changed. My leather cut creaked as I rose from the kneelers and faced the door.

Father Sanchez wasn't wearing his vestments today. Instead, he wore jeans and a blue work shirt. Even at his age, he was still the parish handyman. He stood in the doorway looking ancient and tiny next to the tall, brown-skinned orderly beside him. They each wore the same grim, sympathetic expression.

"I thought I might find you here," Father said.

"Mr. Wade?" The orderly cleared his throat and stepped into the chapel. "They're ready for you if ... if you're ready."

Ready. Ready? Father Sanchez's eyes held a disappointed sadness as he looked me up and down. I knew what he saw.

At least ... I knew what he wanted to see. By now, it should have been *me* standing next to that orderly looking to shepherd some grieving family member toward the metal double doors at the end of the hall. To him, I should be wearing the collar. He should be sitting in a rocking chair sipping wine and reading one of his favorite doorstopper biographies of one of the founding fathers or revolutionaries.

His eyes settled on the patch on my left breast, his mouth twitching ever so slightly. Only someone who knew him well would have even noticed. I did. My white patch showed the road name my club brothers had given me along with my position among them. "Deacon, Club Chaplain." I had no congregation anymore. I gave no sermons. Now I was the man the rest of the Dark Saints M.C. looked to as their moral compass. That might be the biggest irony of all after what I'd done.

"Yeah," I said, coming out of the pews. Behind Sanchez and the orderly, the door opened into the main hospital. To the right, behind the double steel doors, was the long corridor to the morgue.

Father Sanchez stood almost a foot shorter than me now, arthritis in his spine giving him a hunched back. The orderly wore a patch of his own, a square plastic ID badge that read "Clyde." I didn't know if it was his first or last name.

"Are you sure there isn't someone else we can call?" Father asked. The moment he said it, his lips pursed and I knew he wasn't sure he'd like my answer. I had no family anymore. Not the kind he meant. My father was long dead. My mother was on this very campus in a nursing care facility, her mind ravaged by dementia. My brother ... well ... that's why I was here.

"This way," Clyde said. "Let me tell you what to expect."

"I know what to expect," I said. I'd done this all before. Ten years ago. Same corridor. Same priest by my side. If I closed my eyes, I could see my father's blue lips and white skin as they pulled the drape away from his face. "Let's just get this over with."

Even Father Sanchez gasped at the hard brevity of my reply. I felt guilty, but not for the reasons he wanted.

We went through those cold steel doors. Clyde asked Father to wait in a row of chairs along the wall. It was in me to ask him to go. Partly because I couldn't stand that damn look of pity in his eyes. But mostly because I didn't want this darkness to touch him. In his mind, it had already taken me. And it had taken the man behind this last set of doors, no matter who he was.

So five minutes later, I stood in front of a long, rectangular table. Clyde held his fingers on the zipper clasp of a black body bag. He gave me a quick nod, signaling he was ready to go. So was I.

The sound of the zipper opening echoed. Clyde was quick, efficient, careful as he pulled the black plastic away. I stepped forward and looked inside.

I don't know what other people do. I can't imagine the gutshot feeling parents get when called to do this. I'd seen that plenty. In another life, I had been there to hold their hands afterward, to pray with them, to counsel them. Just like Father Sanchez wanted to do with me. I knew I wouldn't need it.

"Do you recognize him?" Clyde asked, his voice a flat monotone.

"Yeah," I said. "That's Sean. Sean Wade. He's ... he was ... my brother."

The word felt foreign in my mouth as I applied it to the lifeless figure before me. Sean. Two years older than me, people used to think we were twins. He had the same crooked mouth, the same thickness to his nose, though his had been broken at least twice. He looked gray, waxy, not even real. But it was Sean. An old, J-shaped scar cut through the bottom of his chin. He got it playing hockey when he was fourteen years old. His blood had run in a river down his neck and stained the ice.

Clyde was careful. Respectful. He didn't let the bag fall open to show anything above Sean's brow. Sean had been shot in the head, execution-style.

"You're sure?" Clyde asked.

I looked up. A rectangular window opened out into the hallway where two policemen stood, one of them scribbling on a notepad. A speaker affixed to the top corner of the room picked up every word we said.

"I'm sure," I said, aiming my voice straight at the speaker. "This is my brother, Sean Wade. There's no question."

Clyde gave me a grim nod and zipped the body bag closed. He held out his hand, ushering me toward the opposite doorway, the one that would take me into the hall past the police officers.

"Hell of a choice," I muttered. Clyde gave me a sideways glance. Behind door number one, Father Sanchez. Door number two, the cops. They'd want to question me. So would Father. I was in the mood for neither but decided the priest would be less persistent. I had nothing to say to any of them. Not today. Maybe not ever.

I brushed past Clyde and went out the door I came in. Mercifully, Father Sanchez hadn't waited. A wave of relief hit me, then turned quickly to ice as I remembered the P.A. and the code call to the maternity ward. I crossed myself again and headed for the exits.

The early morning air worked its magic on me as I climbed on my Harley and hit the highway going almost eighty. It was just me and the road. The powerful engine rumbled beneath me and I breathed in the tangy salt air of the Gulf as I headed out of town.

I made my way down the winding dirt road to the Dark Saints M.C. clubhouse. For the last two hours, I'd felt almost suspended in time and space, as if I were underwater. Now as Rufus, our club dog, came barreling around the side of the building to greet me, I broke through the surface.

Mama Bear stood in the doorway with her arms crossed. The woman had a sixth sense, I swear ... not unlike the dog. She seemed to know exactly when I'd arrive. I went to her, after giving Rufus the ear scratch he demanded.

"Hey, Mama," I said. She reached up and touched my cheek, her steely eyes creased with concern, far different from pity.

"Hey, yourself," she said. I hugged her quickly; her spiky white hair scratched my chin. For as small as she was, she hugged back with a hell of a grip. "It was him?"

"Yeah."

Her eyes twinkled, but she didn't say the empty things people usually say. Instead, she just rubbed my upper arm and closed the door behind us as I walked into the clubhouse.

She didn't have to tell me where I'd find everyone else. The conference room door was wide open and I could hear our club prez Bear's deep laughter echo through the walls. Sean's death was club business, until it wasn't. I was glad Bear called the rest of the guys. It would save me from having to explain things more than once.

"You want anything?" Mama Bear asked. "Hair of the dog?"

She was kidding. I never drank anything stronger than a sip of church wine or black coffee. I raised a hand behind my head and waved her off as I went into the conference room. It was a different kind of church, but one that often cleansed what was left of my soul just the same.

Bear sat at the head of the table, running his fingers through his thick, white beard. At his side, E.Z., his vice-president, sat, arms crossed, waiting for me to get there. The rest of the guys gave me knowing looks as I took my seat at the other end of the table.

Bear steepled his fingers beneath his chin and looked at me with his cold, hard eyes. Tension ran from him and through every other man at this table as if Bear could set off an electrical current among them with just one breath.

Shep, Bo, Domino, Kade, Maddox, Axle, Benz, Chase, Zig, E.Z., and Bear himself. My brothers. My surrogate father. My family. They meant more to me now than Sean had in years. I lost ... no ... I gave up the family I was born into to join this one. I knew from the flicker in Bear's eyes he was thinking about the reasons why today just as I was. Sean had left me no choice.

They were all looking to me. None of them would come out and ask it. This wasn't how this was supposed to go. I was the one who would seek them out when I knew some fabric of their lives had ripped apart. They came to me looking for absolution, to confess when the light we fought for was touched by the darkness we had to dance with.

"It's okay," I said, trying to break the tension. "I mean ... I am. It was Sean. But we already knew that."

Bear let out a hard sigh and dropped his gaze from me for a moment. I was itching to talk to him alone, so was he. He and E.Z. passed a glance. They were the only two people at this table who knew the truth about Sean and me. The rest only guessed or knew well enough not to ask.

"Cops are saying he was found in the alley behind Digby's," E.Z. said. "Did you talk to them?"

It felt like both a question and an accusation. If I hadn't been staring at Shep when he said it, I might not have picked up on a second undercurrent running around the table. Shep looked at Bo. Bo looked at Axle. I knew them well enough to guess there was something they each wanted to say.

"No," I answered. "Didn't want anything to do with them. When they want to talk to me, they know where to find me."

"Good instincts," Bear said. "And we don't have any solid reason to connect this shit to the club anyway."

"Are you kidding?" E.Z. said, slamming his fist on the table. "You think it was a coincidence they dumped Sean Wade's body behind Digby's?"

"We don't own Digby's," Chase said. "And it's not the first or last time some drug dealer gets dumped down there. Sorry, Deacon."

I put a hand up to wave off the offense. "Chase's right. This could be a hundred things coming to a head in Sean's life. I hadn't talked to him, hell, I hadn't seen him in almost a year. The last time he came to hit me up for money. I gave it to him. I know I shouldn't have, but he knew it was the last time I ever would. I stuck to it."

"The time before that, he cleaned your mother's house out." Shep said it, his tone grim as he locked eyes with me. It had happened a year and a half ago. When I realized my mother couldn't live on her own anymore, club connections helped me get her into the facility at the Gulfside Nursing Home. She had my brother listed on her paperwork as her health advocate though. They called him. He went in the middle of the night and raided her house for cash, jewelry, and all her appliances. He even stripped out the copper plumbing.

"I've got feelers out," Bear said. "Trying to reconstruct the last few months. See who Sean had been mixing with. Who he owed."

"Everyone," I said.

"He wasn't killed in that alley," E.Z. said. "Jenny says the theory is he was dumped there. That means something. You don't gotta be Nancy Drew to figure this shit out. This was a message. Sean wasn't a member of the club, but the whole damn town knows he was your brother, Deacon. He'd have been dead years ago if not for that. This was the Hawks. And everyone here knows what it means. If they're going after family, then …"

"Deacon cut Sean off years ago," Shep said. "Everyone in this town also knew that."

"Fine," E.Z. said, leveling a withering look at Shep. There was bad blood between those two and it was getting worse. E.Z. was the most closed off to me. He didn't come to me like the men closer to my own age did. Shep was Bear's son. I knew it rattled E.Z. sometimes if Bear deferred to him over E.Z. The truth was, Bear was careful, diplomatic. If anything, he was harder on Shep than the rest of us. Still, the fault lines running through the men at this table had deepened lately and there was no denying it.

"We'll tighten security," Bear said. "No reason not to. Until we know more about Sean's murder, I think it's smart to assume it might have been an indirect message."

"Indirect message?" A purple vein jumped in E.Z.'s temple. Bear put a hand up to silence him. Usually that worked. Not today.

"I say we hit 'em back hard and now!"

For the first time, there were knocks of support around the table. Domino. Zig. Even Chase.

"And I think Bear's right," I said. "My brother had been dealing for the better part of the last decade. He's been addicted to his product for the last couple of years. I think there's too many other solid reasons why someone would have wanted to put a bullet in his head besides club retaliation. We should wait and see, but watch our backs even more in the meantime."

This wasn't a formal vote, just a status meeting, but I knew my words carried weight. Sean Wade had been my blood brother, after all. At least, once upon a time. My gut twisted as I closed my eyes and remembered the last real conversation we'd ever had. He accused me of stealing the only woman he ever loved. It was a lie, but not for the reasons he thought. Sean didn't know how to love for real.

Bear adjourned Church and dismissed everyone. I hung back. So did E.Z. It drew some curious looks from a few of the other guys, but they all filed out into the main room where Mama Bear waited with a huge pot of chili and beer on tap.

Bear sat back in his chair while E.Z. got up to pace. My stomach roiled as I got up and walked to the end of the table. Bear looked up, his expression stony. He knew what I was going to ask even before I said it.

"It has to be me," I said. "I have to be the one to tell her." My words felt so dry in my throat. My heart pumped like a bass drum; I was sure Bear could hear it too.

"It's been a long time. She's bound to have moved on. Built a life for herself. You sure, son?" Bear said. Son. Father Sanchez had called me that today too. Yet with Bear, it felt more real. It didn't feel like a knife twisting in my heart. Ten years had changed so much. But not enough.

"I'm sure." My heart lurched. Could I go back? Could I reopen these wounds and still hold onto what was left of my soul?

"She needs to know what happened. She needs to hear it from me. Do you still know where she is?" I asked. Ten years ago, I'd made the two men in this room swear never to answer that question for me.

Bear lowered his gaze then reached into the breast pocket of his leather cut. He knew. Of course he knew I would ask this. He pulled out a slip of paper. Just a tiny folded square. And yet, I knew what he'd written on it could change the trajectory of my life again. Just like it had ten years ago.

He slipped the paper into my palm, giving me a firm, solid handshake. I withdrew and put the paper into my own breast pocket without looking at it. E.Z.'s eyes were burning through me too. I knew I should thank them both. All these years, they'd done what I asked. Even now, they were doing it when they knew how wrong my decision might be.

"Take a few days, son," Bear said. "But don't disappear."

Nodding, I turned to leave. That tiny slip of paper with an address written on it I'd sworn him never to give me burned right beside my broken heart.

Chapter 2

BETH

"All rise!"

My heart dropped into my three-inch heels as Judge Dupree's bailiff's voice boomed through the courtroom. Judge Tobias Dupree VII flipped his robe around his waist as he took the three short steps up to his bench. He peered at me over horn-rimmed half glasses, his deep scowl cutting through me. I gave him a weak smile and looked behind me.

"Where the hell are you, Eddie?" I muttered through gritted teeth. Judge Dupree ran his docket with military precision. All summary judgment hearings took place at one o'clock sharp on Thursdays. The second hand on the large round clock above the double doors snapped to the twelve at the exact time the judge took his last step.

My throat ran dry as I shuffled the papers on the table in

front of me. All eyes turned to the conspicuously empty chair beside me. I looked down, afraid to make eye contact with the judge or the plaintiff's counsel to my right.

Chairs shuffled as Judge Dupree took his seat. He made a great show out of shuffling his own paperwork. Bless him for trying to stall for even that little bit of time. The courtroom doors behind me stayed ominously closed.

"Miss Kennedy?" Judge Dupree said. I bit my bottom lip, took a breath, and met his withering stare.

"Yes, your Honor." I slowly rose to my feet again as the judge addressed me.

"Is Mr. Albright going to grace us with his presence this afternoon?"

"Uh ... yes, your Honor. He just stepped out for a moment." I was skirting the truth, but not outright lying. Dupree wasn't stupid, he saw right through me.

"Your Honor." Clayton Benedict, counsel for the plaintiff, rose from his chair. "If Mr. Albright can't see fit to show up to argue his own motion, with all due respect, what are the rest of us even doing here?"

Dupree chewed his bottom lip. He was the oldest county judge in the state of Texas. He'd won re-election two days before his seventy-fifth birthday. They'd force him out at the end of his term, but if I knew anything about the Honorable Tobias Dupree VII, he wouldn't go quietly.

I couldn't help but turn back to the doors. I stared hard at them, as if I could will Eddie to appear. Each second that he didn't, I could feel our client's chances slipping away. This motion should be a slam dunk. I researched and wrote it myself, just like I did for all Eddie's cases these days. The plaintiff dropped a bombshell during her deposition. Eddie was defending a local therapist against a negligence claim, only the plaintiff openly admitted the bad deed happened over six years ago. Way beyond the statute of limitations. All Eddie had to do was stand up in court and show that testimony to the judge. It was simple math. I could argue this in my sleep. Except legally, I wasn't allowed. Eddie was the lawyer. I was his paralegal.

"I move to dismiss this motion."

"Your Honor!" My tone came out as more of a shout; the echo of it made even my ears ring. "If we could just have a few more minutes. Mr. Albright wasn't feeling well this morning. Is there any chance we could move this hearing to the end of your docket today?"

Sympathy filled Judge Dupree's face. Even arguing for more time may be overstepping my bounds. But the judge knew Eddie. Everyone in this county did. They also knew full well where I'd likely find him. Ten to one, he was probably pulling up a chair to a different bench right this very minute, the Lonestar Bar just off U.S. 10.

"Miss Kennedy," Judge Dupree said. "Mr. Benedict has a point. This is Mr. Albright's motion. Plaintiff's counsel has taken the trouble to prepare a written response. And they've shown up today. He is ready to proceed with oral argument. Now, unless you've passed the bar in the last five minutes, as competent as you are, I can't allow you to do it for Mr. Albright. In the alternative, is your client here today? He can always argue on his own behalf."

I swallowed hard. The answer was no.

"Fine." Judge Dupree sighed.

"Your Honor, I move to dismiss the defendant's motion and for entry of an order of judgment in the amount specified in the complaint."

It was as if my heart turned to sawdust. I couldn't breathe. Never mind losing the case, this would open Eddie up to malpractice in a best-case scenario. In the worst, he'd lose his license. And so would go my own career and health insurance.

I opened my mouth to object. The hell with not having a law license. I couldn't just stand here and let this happen. But Judge Dupree could pretty much read my mind. He held a hand up to silence me.

"Here's what I'm going to do. I'll hear from the plaintiff's counsel because he at least bothered to show up. You, Miss Kennedy, will sit there quietly and refrain from doing anything else that looks like the unauthorized practice of law. I have written briefs from both parties. I'll rule on them in writing after hearing from Mr. Benedict today."

"Your Honor." Clayton popped up again. As angry as Judge Dupree was at Eddie, he sure didn't like being interrupted. Apparently nobody ever taught Clayton Benedict the lesson of quitting while he was ahead. My heart sank.

"I said I'd hear from you, Mr. Benedict," Dupree said. "I didn't say you could interrupt me."

"I just wanted to put in on record that we're asking for sanctions!"

Dupree dropped his shoulders and slammed back in his seat. "You can *put* that on the record when I tell you it's your turn to talk!"

I sank slowly into my chair, clasped my hands in front of me, and silently prayed that Clayton Benedict would continue to put his foot in his mouth. It was about the only thing that might save Eddie and our client's case at the moment.

My nerves withering, I sat quietly for the next ten minutes listening to Benedict argue his motion defense. It had about a million holes in it and I had to literally bite my tongue to keep from pointing them out. It was torture. When he finished, he sat back down and glared at me with his chest puffed out.

"That's it?" Dupree asked.

"Yes, your Honor," Benedict answered.

"Then we're adjourned. Miss Kennedy? Go find your boss and tell him I'd like to see him in my chambers at five o'clock. And do me a favor."

"Anything, your Honor," I said, rising as he spoke to me.

Dupree pushed his glasses back up his nose. "I take that back. Do us *all* a favor, Miss Kennedy: get a law license already."

He banged his gavel and left the bench in a swirl of black fabric. My feet barely touched the ground as I gathered Eddie's file and ran out the back of the courtroom. Benedict shouted after me, but I didn't stop. If Eddie was where I knew we all believed he was, I only had a couple of hours to find him, help him dry out, and get him back to the courthouse to meet with Dupree.

Mercifully, I'd gotten a good parking spot right in front of Crystal Falls District Court. I zoomed out of town and went straight to the Lonestar. Sure enough, Eddie's silver Pontiac was parked at an angle next to the building. As usual, he left the keys tucked under the driver's side wheel well. I grabbed them and ran into the bar.

Eddie was sitting in his usual end stool, regaling the bartender with courtroom war stories from his last thirty years of practice. Half of them were even true. Sadie, the bar's owner, saw me come in and shook her head as she flipped two beer mugs upright, ready to fill them.

"Ed!" As I reached the end of the bar, the patron sitting in the stool beside Eddie vacated it for me. Everyone here knew this drill by heart.

Eddie's eyes went in and out of focus as I took the seat beside him and tugged on his sleeve. Eddie was dressed for court, at least wearing his tan suit with the suede elbow patches. His white hair stuck out in peaks. His bulbous nose was nearly purple and his wiry eyebrows twitched as he looked at me.

"Ed," I said, trying not to raise my voice. "Time to get you out of here. You've got a meeting with Judge Dupree. You forgot about the Grayson summary judgment hearing. They held it without you."

I made a sweeping gesture across my neck to Morris, the bartender. He was Ed's age, mid-fifties. They'd gone to high school together. Morris nodded but he also knew the drill. He'd probably cut Eddie off a few rounds ago. Which meant I was sure to find a silver flask of Bourbon in his suit jacket.

"There she is!" Ed Albright, Esquire shouted. "Beth Kennedy. My girl Friday. The girl with no past!"

My heart sank. This little speech meant on a scale of one to ten, Eddie was an eight and a half. He'd still be piss drunk in two hours. No way I could present him to Judge Dupree like this. I'd need to stall for time.

"Give it a rest, Ed, will ya?" Sadie called from the other end of the bar. Bless her. "Leave the kid alone. Still can't figure out why she even puts up with your bullshit. I hope you're paying her well."

He was. That was the truth of it. Eddie hadn't drawn a salary for himself in over five years. He didn't need it. I found him nine years ago at a low point in my own life. I'd read about a case he was trying in the *Crystal Falls Gazette*. A products liability case against a baby formula company. Two infant twins had died. I took a chance, suspecting he'd need research help and grunt work. I was right. He eventually won the case. His share was over five million dollars. Enough to afford me and my health insurance.

I took a chance on him, but he took a bigger chance on me.

The girl with no past. Just like he said. No resume or references either. I couldn't even give him my last address. I'd done my level best to save him from himself ever since. But he'd saved me just as much.

"Come on," I said. "We'll tell Judge Dupree you've come down with the stomach flu. He might even buy it this time."

"A supermodel on the lam," he said, drawing even more open-mouthed stares from the bar patrons and Morris and Sadie.

"Not even close, Ed," I said. It did me no good to let Eddie draw attention to me this way. I just hoped they'd write it off as the rantings of a drunk.

"Former C.I.A.," he said.

"Nope." I tucked a hand under Eddie's elbow and gently pulled him off the stool. I lifted my chin toward Morris and slapped a twenty-dollar bill on the bar, hoping it was enough to put a dent in Eddie's tab.

"K.G.B?"

"Getting warmer." I smiled. This was an old game between us. For now, it would keep him focused on something other than the fact that I was leading him out of the bar and into my Ford pick-up. If he saw his own car, he might resist and argue that he was fine to drive.

"Former Russian ice skater. You defected to the U.S. after winning a silver medal in a heartbreaking tie to an East German skater in the last Olympics."

"Good guess," I said. "But East Germany hasn't existed since I was in, I don't know, preschool?"

"Damn. I thought that was it for sure. I know ... circus performer. You're on the lam after a torrid affair with a Romanian trapeze artist. Broke up his marriage."

I sighed. "Come on, Eddie. Time to quit while you're behind." I put a hand on his head to protect it, cop-style, as Eddie climbed into the passenger seat of my truck. He could come back for his Pontiac tomorrow or I'd call in a favor to Mickey Weller, owner of the only body shop in Crystal Falls. He could tow it back in exchange for Eddie's waiving his legal bill on some collections work we did for him last year. It wouldn't be the first time and likely not the last.

By the time I hit the highway again, Eddie had slumped over in his seat. He drooled against my window and snored loud as a freight train. My heart sank. I'd never be able to get him out of the truck in that condition without some help.

I turned up the radio and listened to some classic country. Eddie kept on snoring. Judge Dupree's words rang in my head. *Do us all a favor and get your law license.* God, if only I could. But like Eddie said, I was the girl with no past. I could probably get into law school as Beth Kennedy. I knew I could pass the bar in my sleep. I just couldn't risk the scrutiny of the mandatory background check I'd have to endure before they'd issue me a bar card.

So I would stay Beth Kennedy, crackerjack paralegal. Girl Friday to Eddie Albright, one of the most brilliant lawyers in the state when he was sober. Hell, even when he was half in the bag. He took me for who I was. Just like I did for him. And on we would go.

I pulled into the office parking lot. The law offices of Edward Albright were housed in a pale green Victorian farmhouse on the outskirts of Crystal Falls. The place was a historic landmark. President Van Buren had once stayed here.

I climbed out and went to the passenger door. Eddie was still slumped against it, drooling. I checked my phone. It was quarter after three. I pressed my own forehead against the glass, meeting Eddie's.

"You're killing me," I said. What in God's name was I going to tell Judge Dupree?

"You're enabling him!" Darlene Albright slammed the front door behind her as she waddled down the ramp. She was Eddie's older sister and secretary.

"I'm trying to keep him from a malpractice lawsuit. With any luck, Judge Dupree will be satisfied with the merits of the brief we submitted on the Grayson case."

Darlene flapped her hands. Her cheeks were flushed as she reached the end of the ramp. Her brother's physical ailments were mostly of his own making. Too much booze. Too much sugar and fried foods. Darlene was born with hers. Standing only four foot eight due to a painfully twisted spine, she walked with a swinging limp. Her wiry gray hair flew in all directions as she shook an accusatory finger at her brother.

"Oh, I know everything, honey. Misty called me before you even left the courthouse." Of course she did. With a population just north of six thousand people, everyone knew everyone's business in Crystal Falls. Misty was the head court clerk. Before I came along, she did more to keep Eddie upright than anyone. They'd been engaged years ago. She'd never admit it, but Misty Loomis still carried an Olympic-sized torch for Eddie Albright. God help her.

"Might as well get him inside," Darlene said. She brushed past me and swung the car door open. I gasped as Eddie slumped over and spilled to the ground. The fall barely fazed him. Darlene delivered a light kick to his ribs. Not enough to hurt him, just enough to let him know she was there.

Eddie smiled up at his big sister and miraculously hauled himself to his feet. His eyes sparkled and for a moment, I had hoped I could get him to his meeting with the judge after all.

"You have a visitor," Darlene said, shouting over her shoulder to me. "I told him to leave, but the bugger's persistent. Not from around here."

An engine revved in the side parking lot. My heart plummeted as the familiar sound cut through me. It couldn't be. I was hearing things. I half turned, catching a glimpse of the gleaming chrome of the Harley's handlebars.

No.

I couldn't think. I couldn't move.

"I told you to wait inside!" Darlene shouted. Eddie was up under his own power now. He dusted off his trousers and swung an arm around Darlene.

The Harley pulled up alongside us. My eyes went up and up. My mouth gaped open and I took a step back. I saw my stunned reflection in the rider's mirrored aviator glasses until he slowly slipped them down his nose.

Those eyes. Pale blue, dark-rimmed irises. His hair was different. Long on top but shaved at the sides. He looked rougher, meaner, hardened. He swung one denim-clad leg over the bike and tucked his sunglasses into the collar of his white t-shirt.

"Beth?" he asked. His voice rippled through me.

"Danny," I whispered, trembling.

I was the girl with no past. But with the revving of Danny Wade's motorcycle engine, my past had just caught up with me.

Chapter 3

Deacon

I saw her through a kind of tunnel vision. She was there, right in front of me. And yet, she felt so far away. It all happened within the span of a few seconds, but in my mind, an eternity played out. No. Not an eternity. Ten years.

I still couldn't believe it. All this time, E.Z. and Bear had only sent Beth a hundred and fifty miles away. Crystal Falls, Texas, just outside of San Antonio. It was a quick ride up U.S.10 and one I'd made hundreds of times in the last decade. Hell, I'd even stopped here once or twice. There was a greasy spoon just off the highway. We used it as a meeting place every once in a while.

I wanted to rail and rage that she was too close. The enemies I'd tried to protect her from could have easily tracked her this close to Port Azrael. But they hadn't. She was here. Alive. Safe, from what I could tell.

"Everything all right, Beth?" My neck snapped around. A crumpled, middle-aged guy stumbled out of the truck Beth had been driving. He wore a tan suit with patches on the elbows. His pot belly hung over his belt and his dark brown tie flapped in the wind. A sign swung on a wooden post in the front of the building. It read "Law Offices of Edward Albright."

"It's ... it's okay, Eddie," Beth said. My heart flipped over. Her voice. I heard it in my dreams sometimes. But she was real, standing twenty feet in front of me. Her brown eyes locked with mine.

"Come on, Ed, let's get some food into you." I'd barely noticed the other woman standing at the end of an access ramp in front of the old farmhouse. She was wide and short. She walked with a pronounced limp, but her grip was strong when she grabbed Edward Albright by the arm and led him into the building. She cast a worried glance back at Beth, but whisked her charge away with swift purpose.

A beat passed. Then another. Beth stood in front of her truck, gripping her keys between her fingers. She looked exactly the same and yet completely different. She wore a black business suit that showed off her shapely legs in high black heels. Her hair was the same, brown with honey highlights in the sun. She still wore it long past her shoulders with bangs swept to the side. Her eyes still cut through me beneath the thick arch of her brow. Those lips, full and soft in a permanent pout. If I closed my eyes, I could still feel the lingering taste of her.

I snapped my eyes open and shook off the memory. My body still remembered her. I felt the echoes of her touch. Even now, it made my dick tighten to be this close to her. Her face was different, more mature and beautiful. The youthful blush on her cheeks had vanished, replaced by something even more sensual. Her cheekbones seemed higher. Tiny laugh lines near her eyes made them sparkle even more than I remembered. Jealousy gripped my heart. I wanted to be the one to make her laugh.

"Danny." My name quivered on her lips. It was all she'd ever called me. It didn't fit anymore. I cut my engine and swung off the bike. Her eyes darted over me and her breath hitched as I came toward her.

"It's Deacon now," I said. "Nobody ever calls me Danny."

Her eyes went up and up, staying locked with mine. Beth. Sweet Beth. My greatest temptation. My brother's wife.

"What are you doing here?" She put a hand to her cheek. "How did you even find me?"

I watched the tiniest flicker in her eyes as she realized the answer before I gave it. "Is there somewhere we can talk?" I asked.

She took a faltering step back. We were pretty much out in the middle of nowhere. Crystal Falls itself was a podunk town with maybe one streetlight and an old-fashioned downtown that looked like it had been ripped right out of the fifties and frozen in time. Of all the places Bear and E.Z. could have sent her, I still couldn't believe they picked this one. Or that she'd agreed to stay.

No sooner had I thought it, I knew why. She'd stayed here

because once upon a time she trusted me. She believed me when I told her this was the only way to keep her safe. I knew now that was only half true.

She turned and opened the cab of her truck. Gesturing to the passenger side, she climbed in. I did a quick scan of the road. The law offices of Edward Albright were located this side of nowhere. Though I'd have rather parked my bike somewhere less conspicuous, I didn't figure many people came down this way unless they were looking for the place. But Beth didn't start the truck.

Shrugging, I took her meaning. She was right. Her truck was probably as good a place as any to have this conversation. I climbed in next to her and turned in the seat to face her.

I watched her trying to process everything before I'd even really spoken a word. While she looked so much like the last time I saw her, I knew I looked anything but. Her eyes traveled down, taking in the leather cut, the patch I wore.

"Club chaplain," she said, her voice breaking. She reached for me, but it was as if we were separated by glass. In a way, we were. We looked at each other as if we were both museum pieces. Look. Don't touch.

"I told you I could never go back," I said.

Hurt flashed in her eyes, then was quickly replaced with anger. "Do you blame me for that?"

Her words reached me with the force of a physical slap. "No!" I said, almost shouting it. "No." Quieter this time. "Beth ..." I stopped. The club had given her a new identity. A place to start her life over. It only now just occurred to me the woman on the access ramp had also called her Beth.

"I didn't know you were here until two days ago," I started again. "I made Bear and E.Z. swear never to tell me. Only that they promised to keep you safe. And you are, aren't you?"

There were tears threatening to fall from her eyes. I wanted to reach for her and wipe them away.

"Yes," she said. "I'm safe. And I do have a life here."

"But your name."

"Beth," she answered before I could say it. "I'm Beth Kennedy now. Your people said it would be easier, safer if we kept some things the same. It still doesn't feel right though. I still catch myself when people call me Ms. Kennedy. I have to force myself to answer. Isn't that funny? I've lived as Beth Kennedy three times longer than I lived as Beth Wade. But my married name fit me so quickly. I've never been able to figure out why that is. I mean, it's just a name, right?"

She was babbling. She did that when she was nervous. My heart warmed that there was at least one thing about her that hadn't changed. This was Beth. *My* Beth. That old desire flared through me as I formed the words in my head. My Beth. Except that kind of thinking is what led us both down the path to destruction all those years ago.

"It's not so strange," I said.

"What are you doing here, Danny?"

"Deacon," I corrected her. Her old name may still be more comfortable, but mine wasn't.

"I just can't believe it," she said. For a moment, it didn't feel like she was talking to me. It seemed more like she was talking to herself, trying to come to grips with the fact I was here.

"Which part?" I asked.

She reached for me again. This time, she ran her fingers over the outline of my patch. "I guess I thought after we ... after I was out of your life, you'd change your mind. That you'd go back. Oh, Danny ... why didn't you? Father Sanchez would have taken you back. He would have understood. What happened was ... God. They weren't normal circumstances. You could have continued on. Taken your Holy Orders ..."

When she reached up to touch my face, I closed my fingers around her wrist. "Don't." Her eyes widened, then she pulled her hand away from me and folded it in her lap. It took everything in me not to touch her again.

"I'm not here to rehash any of that," I said. "I've chosen my path. It's long past time for looking back." The words came out of my mouth, but I wasn't sure if I was saying them for her benefit or mine.

"Fine," she said, turning cold on me. I deserved that and a lot worse.

"I came to tell you," I started again. I'd rehearsed this little speech a thousand times on the ride out here; now that it came time to utter it, a knife twisted in my heart. I'm not sure what I was more afraid of. That my words would hurt Beth, or that she'd moved on to a point they couldn't.

"No," she said. "I'm not going through this again. I've already given everything up once. I started over. There was a time I didn't think I could. It was hard ... Deacon. Harder than you can possibly imagine. I guess you did too, but you got to do it from the comfort of your own home. Surrounded by people who knew you. I was alone. So whatever Sean's done this time, whatever he's gotten mixed up in, I'm not going to run from it anymore. I'm through paying for his mistakes. And I'm through paying for yours."

The speech I'd planned crumbled into dust as Beth stared at me with those wide, brown eyes. She was right. She'd always been right. She alone had been the innocent in all of this. But she'd been the one to lose the most.

"So?" she said, tapping her fingers on the steering wheel. "Why don't you just get it over with? Tell me what you came here for. What's Sean done?"

I took a breath, squared my shoulders and delivered the news I knew would shatter her hard-won peace all over again.

"Beth, Sean's dead. Last week. Someone shot him in the head. I came to tell you that you're free."

Chapter 4

Beth

I couldn't think. I couldn't breathe. Danny was talking but it was as if I could only process every third word he said. Maybe even less. I watched him, focusing on the tiniest details of him. His hands were broad and strong, rough and calloused. He was bigger than I remembered. Hard muscles rippled through his arms. He wore a white t-shirt under that leather biker vest. It stretched tight over his biceps.

I drew in a breath and closed my eyes. Dead. Free. Sean was dead. I gripped the steering wheel. When I opened my eyes, I focused on Danny's lips. He was still talking, saying words I'd dreamt about once upon a time.

"It's over, Beth. He can't touch you anymore."

Touch me? Danny sat just a few feet from me. He draped one arm over the back of the seat, his fingers just inches from my hair. *He* hadn't laid a finger on me, and yet his presence touched my very core. How many times had I drawn comfort from those arms, his whispered words against my ear? All those nights when I was scared to death my life would crash around me. It was Danny who held me up and helped me find the strength to keep going.

I buried my face in my hands. It was all just too much. Sean was dead. My husband was dead. Danny said I was free. Finally, I got my head clear enough to ask the questions I knew he expected.

"How?"

Danny's eyes flickered. Maybe he'd already told me that. I don't know. Everything was just so jumbled up inside of me. "Somebody shot him in the head, Beth."

I nodded, then rubbed my hands down my skirt, smoothing out the wrinkles. "Was it the cartel?"

Danny rubbed his chin with his thumb, considering his answer. I knew even now he was trying to protect me.

"He was still knee deep with them, wasn't he?" I asked. Tears stung my eyes. Even now, after all these years, it was hard to admit in words what Sean was. He was a drug dealer. My tormentor. For years, I hadn't wanted to believe it. I'd been so naive. We were only eighteen when we got married. I had stars in my eyes over him. I saw Sean in my mind's eye as he'd been that day he drove me to the courthouse. Strong. Handsome. Virile. He'd made me a thousand promises. He had money. Security. He'd offered me a lifeline out of the hellhole I grew up in and I grabbed it with both hands. I just didn't know at the time I was stepping into a different one.

"We hadn't talked in over a year," Danny said. Danny. Deacon. I couldn't stop staring at the patch on his leather vest. Danny was a Dark Saint. I still wasn't sure I believed it. I could blink my eyes and still see him wearing church robes and ministering to the sick on Sundays. He wasn't ordained, but one night long ago, I'd made him hear my confession. Neither of us had ever been the same since.

"But yeah," he said. "He'd been moving up the ranks over the years. We chased him out of town at least half a dozen times but he kept turning back up. A few months ago, he tossed my mom's house."

My stomach flipped. "Was she hurt?" No. God, no. I couldn't bear to hear it. We'd made so many sacrifices to get out from under Sean Wade's dark choices.

"She wasn't home," Danny said. "She's not ... she's got dementia, Beth. I'd made arrangements to move her into a home. Sean caught wind of it and got into the house."

It was involuntary. If I'd taken half a second to think it through, I never would have reached for him. But I did. I pressed my palm to Danny's cheek. Electric fire sparked between us and he squeezed his eyes shut, bracing through it.

He brought his hand up, gently circled my wrist, and drew my hand away. His eyes glinted with pain as they met mine. It was still there. The pain he'd endured all those years ago when he came to me one night in anguished despair. It hadn't left. Being near me brought it all back up.

I folded my hands in my lap and leveled a hard stare at him. "Was this retaliation then? Did the club take care of him?"

Danny's eyes narrowed. In the span of a second, he became something else. It was as if the man I used to know faded away and now I could only see the man he truly was. It was just like he said. Danny was gone. He was Deacon now, member of the Dark Saints, M.C.

"No," he said. "I did not have my own brother killed. Though it's not like I hadn't thought about it a hundred times over the last ten years. But no. This wasn't the Saints."

"So it *was* the cartel then? Sean finally bit the hand that fed him, or whatever?"

Deacon shrugged.

"What aren't you telling me?" I asked. Ten years. He was a different man than the one I knew. I was a different woman too though, wasn't I? And yet, I *did* know this man. I knew the pain in his eyes. I understood the hardness. I'd witnessed the things that put it there.

"Deacon," I said. The sound of his new name coming from my lips seemed to startle him. Then he settled into it, lifting his eyes to mine.

"I'm telling you everything you need to know, Beth. Sean is dead. Whatever ties he had to you are gone. You're safe. He can't hurt you. He won't come after you. The cartel has no reason to do it either. I just wanted you to know that. I wanted to answer the questions I knew you'd have. I wanted you to hear it from me. So that I could tell you ..."

"Tell me what?" My tone turned sharp. A flood of emotions poured from me. I couldn't sort through them. Anger. Relief. Sadness. Grief. I settled on a kind of rage. Even if Danny didn't deserve to bear the brunt of it, it gave me a sense of control I desperately needed.

"Beth ..."

"No! Tell me what? Exactly what am I supposed to do with this?"

"Beth, I'm trying to ..."

I slammed my palm against the steering wheel. The horn gave a sharp blast, drawing Darlene to the front window. She'd probably been watching the whole time. Nervous laughter bubbled up inside of me. What in the hell was I going to tell her?

"Fine," I said, trying desperately hard to hold on to my anger. I didn't want to show it to Danny. It had taken me ten years to form a hard, protective shell around my heart. I couldn't afford any cracks in it now.

"You've told me," I said. "Thank you. But now, what do you want me to do with it? Sean can't hurt me anymore. Can you honestly sit there with a straight face and tell me this ends things? I haven't seen Sean in ten years, but I don't need to know he never changed. If the cartel killed him, it's because he owed them something. It didn't seem to take you much to find me after all this time. What makes you think they won't be next?"

Danny's face turned stone cold. For a moment, all traces of the man I used to know vanished. Gone were his kind eyes, his warm smile. Something hard and dangerous rose up in its place. Even now, I wanted to reach for him and run my fingers through his thick brown hair. The new style, shaved on the sides, made him look rougher, meaner, and yet still devastatingly handsome.

And there was still enough of Sean in him to make my heart skip. Years ago, I told myself that's what drew me to him at first. I truly loved Sean Wade once upon a time. Then he hurt me and warped my love into a weapon he used against me. In Danny, I could almost see the promise of what could have been. Where Sean was hard and evil, Danny was pure and good. Only Sean had twisted that goodness too.

Danny reached for me. He grabbed me by the shoulders, his skin searing mine. He turned me to face him. "No one is going to hurt you. Not ever again. I made you a promise ten years ago. I told you to trust me. I'm telling you you still can. You are under my protection. The cartel knows that. And *no one* knows where you are except for two other men I trust with my life."

I blanched. "And you trust them with mine?"

Danny swallowed. A vein jumped in his temple. "Yes. God ... Beth ... yes."

A single tear fell from my eye. Danny watched the track of it down my cheek. "So now you take the Lord's name in vain, Deacon Wade?"

He didn't move. Not even to breathe. "It's the least of my sins, Beth. You of all people know that."

His words cut straight through me. The thing is, I could believe he hadn't meant to hurt me with them. But the moment they took to the air, he saw my pain reflected back at him.

"So that's it, then," I said. His hands still burned through me where he gripped my shoulders. A different kind of heat melted my insides. Ten years. Ten minutes. It didn't matter. Danny "Deacon" Wade still had the power to turn my world upside down.

"Fallen angel," I said, hating that I wanted to hurt him with my words now too. "Is that it? Yes. We both know I'm your greatest sin."

A storm swirled through my heart, threatening to rip it in half. I'd dreamt of this day so many times. What would it feel like to be close to Danny again? Surely the years and distance should have given us both perspective. We'd both been so lost the last time I saw him. He'd lost his father. I'd finally understood how dangerous Sean really was.

"No," Danny said, his eyes cold as ice. "You're many things to me, Beth. But you are *not* my greatest sin."

In that moment, I believed him. Pain etched deep lines on his face. God help me, but I wanted to try and kiss them away. One desperate night a million years ago, I had. My body still ached from the memory of the pleasure we took from each other.

"Danny," I whispered, touching his cheek. For a moment, he sank into my touch, his eyes squeezing shut. Then they snapped open and the ice came back. We let each other go.

"Deacon," I said with cold resolve. "So you made your deal with the devil, is that it? You finally realized the church couldn't save you so you traded in your collar for that cut?"

I traced the outline of the white patch at his breast. Deacon reached up and pulled my hand away. "I wanted to make sure you'd be okay."

I wasn't sure if he meant now or then. Was he telling me he joined the M.C. for *me* in some twisted way? I wasn't sure I could hear the answer just then. It was all too much.

"I'm okay," I said. "I have a life."

Something changed in Danny's face when I said it. As if he had another, deeper question he was afraid to ask. I realized I was harboring the same curiosity. What *was* Danny's life now? Was he happy? Did he have someone? Oh yes, for now I was also afraid to ask.

"Thank you," I said, opening the door beside me. Danny gave me a tight-lipped smile and climbed out of the cab.

As I stepped down to the ground, I hugged my arms around me. I took a few tentative steps, following Danny to his bike. He slid on his aviator glasses and climbed on the Harley. There was still that secret, reckless part of me that wanted to know what it would feel like to climb on behind him, wrap my arms around his waist, and let the road fly under us.

"What I told you is true," Danny ... Deacon said as he settled into his seat. "No one is going to come looking for you, Beth. Sean's shit can't touch you anymore. You can live your life the way you want now. No more looking over your shoulder."

I nodded. There was little else I could say. "Take care of yourself, Danny ... er ... Deacon."

Danny revved his engine and the roar of it kickstarted my heart. He gave me one last glance before he pulled out of the driveway and zoomed down the road, leaving me breathless and shattered in his wake.

Chapter 5

Deacon

Dust. That's all that was left of my brother. On a sweltering July day, a week after I last saw Beth, I spread Sean's ashes over our father's grave. When it was finished, I leaned down and traced the lettering on my old man's headstone.

Coleman Wade. Loving husband, devoted father. Rest easy in the arms of the Lord.

Dad had bought a family plot not long after Sean and I were born. Someday soon, I would lay my mother to rest beside him. Today, I just couldn't bear to put Sean in the ground next to him. There was no one left who could make these decisions but me.

"I'm sorry, Dad," I said, making the sign of the cross. If he looked down on me today, he wouldn't rest easy. He might have expected his other son to wear a Dark Saints cut, but never me. The last thing he knew, I was two weeks from taking my Holy Orders. Then one horrible night, everything changed.

I kissed the headstone and walked back to my Harley. Thoughts of Beth swam in my head today as the sun nearly blinded me. If I'd asked her to do this with me, would she have said yes? Would I have wanted her to? Part of me needed to see Sean the way I did so I could close a door. I'd spent so many years trying to protect Beth, maybe she needed that closure too.

I took the coastal highway on the outskirts of town. The Gulf air filled my soul and helped me settle as I turned down the back roads toward the clubhouse. Though everyone had given me space over the last week, Bear wanted me back. Sean's murder was still an open question that put everyone on edge.

I parked in the back and headed into the bar. Shep and Axle were the only ones in the main room. Mid-afternoon on a Sunday, they shared a pitcher of beer between them while Mama Bear cleaned behind the bar. Shep and Axle sat grim-faced as I headed into the back rooms looking for Bear. There was something up between those two. They'd been acting weird for the better part of a month. When I asked Mama about it before Sean's death, she shrugged it off, saying things were just tense lately. I knew it was something else, but didn't press. My own plate was full.

"You doing all right, son?" Bear asked. He sat with his feet up on the conference table, one booted foot over the other. E.Z. paced on one end. He gestured with his chin and I closed the door behind me.

"All good, Bear," I answered.

"Did you break the news to your mother?" Bear asked.

I gave him a shrug. "I tried. She seemed to understand for about thirty seconds. Then she got this glassy stare and a faraway smile. She started talking to me like she thought I was my dad. After a while, it was just easier to let her think that. It made her ... happy. That woman's been through enough in her life. She deserved peace, even if it's a product of her Swiss cheese mind."

"Don't we all," Bear said. "Sit down, Deacon."

My gut twisted. I didn't like his tone one bit. But I did as he asked. E.Z. kept on pacing and it rattled me.

"The news isn't good," Bear finally said. "I've put some feelers out. Jenny's fed me some intel from the investigation. She's putting her ass on the line a bit over it, you know that?"

Jenny was Benz's girl. A detective with the Port Az P.D., she helped us when she could. Though I knew she'd never compromise an active investigation or her own morals. Then again, my own moral compass had shifted the day I joined this club. I wouldn't change it. It had taken me years to sort that out, but this club was in my blood now more than the priesthood ever could have been. That was the deepest secret I kept.

"I know," I said. "And tell her I appreciate it."

"She knows that. Look, Deacon, the cops just can't get to the bottom of Sean's murder. The way he was hit, we all know he was executed. And it wasn't random. Crime scene guys have figured out Sean wasn't shot in that alley behind Digby's. He was dumped there after the fact."

My heart lurched. It's what I was afraid of. There could be no question someone had been trying to send a message to the club. The question was, who?

"So we're back to square one, it's the cartel or it's the Hawks," I said, pounding my fist on the table.

A look passed between E.Z. and Bear that told me they were already leaning one way. As I sat there, I honestly didn't know which would be worse. If this was the Devils Hawks, our main club rival, it meant they wanted war and they weren't planning on following any code. They'd targeted a family member, even though Sean was far from innocent. On the other hand, if this was the cartel, it meant Beth's fears could be well founded. Even after all these years, they might try to find her to collect any outstanding debt Sean owed them.

"How's Beth?" Bear asked, damn near reading my mind.

I nodded. "You were right. She's got a life. She seemed good. A little shaken, what with seeing me and everything I told her. But she's good."

I knew I wasn't telling Bear anything he didn't already know. Beth's safety was the promise he'd made me all those years ago when I came to him for help. It was well worth the price of my soul.

"Good," Bear said. E.Z.'s silence unsettled me. He was sweating a little at the temples. Even from here, I could see his chest heaving. Something had gone down between these two before I walked in the door. It might even explain the weird vibe I got out of Axle and Shep in the main bar. I didn't like any of it one damn bit.

"Listen," I said. "You've gotta have a feel for this. Both of you. You've been around longer than any of the rest of us. What do you think this is? Is it the Hawks spoiling for war? I mean, they had to know Sean was already dead to me. If they wanted to send this kind of a message, don't you think they would have picked somebody, I don't know, closer?"

"You wishing they did?" E.Z.'s clipped voice cut through me. The outburst didn't seem to fit the circumstances. I kept my cool. It wasn't worth the aggravation. I put a hand up, gesturing surrender.

"That's not what I'm saying," I said. "I'm just trying to look at all the angles, same as you."

"We need to bring this to the full membership," E.Z. said; clearly this had been part of what they'd been arguing about before I got here. Bear would counsel caution, E.Z. was ready to fight. The truth was, I didn't know what side I fell on. I *did* know a war vote would probably split the club right down the middle if E.Z. forced the issue.

"And we will," Bear said, giving E.Z. an arched brow. He didn't change his casual posture. "But first, we need more concrete information. It sure as hell smells like the Hawks, but Sean didn't have clean hands and we all know it. I'm not saying he deserved what he got ..."

I put a hand up, this time to placate Bear. "Don't. Not on my account. I'm the last person who needs to be reminded of what my brother was. And I've lost too many people I care about because of the choices he made."

"What do you want to do, son?" Bear said, leveling an intense stare at me.

I chewed my bottom lip. I hadn't been able to get Beth out of my mind since the moment the cops called to tell me about Sean. "I'd like your permission to light out of here for a little while to look after some family business."

Bear's face fell. "I kinda figured you'd say that."

"Two birds, one stone," I said. "It'll give me peace of mind to see with my own eyes that Beth's good. That she's safe. If this *was* the cartel and that bullet didn't finish the business they had with Sean, then she needs eyes on her for a little while. If they're going to make a move, it'll be sooner rather than later. And if they *do* make a move on her, then we'll know for sure what's going on."

"I'm not going to lie," Bear said. "I don't like the idea of you being off by yourself. Not with things in a state of flux like they are. Why don't you take Toby or one of the other probies with you to watch your back?"

I shrugged off his concerns. "That'll spook her. You don't know Beth like I do. And if things go the way I plan them, she won't even know I'm there. She's been safe all these years and I think that's in large part because you're the only other people in the world who knew where she was. Changing that now would be too much of a risk if Sean's business is about to catch up with her again."

Bear nodded. I knew he couldn't argue my logic. "Fine," he said. "I'll give you a few days. But Deacon, you check in with me regularly. If your phone rings, it's gonna be me or E.Z., and you need to answer it. And if I decide I don't want you down there without eyes in the back of your head and send some your way, you don't shake 'em. You got it?"

I leaned across the table. "Fair enough."

"What are you planning on telling the other guys?" E.Z. asked, scowling.

I rose and slapped his shoulder. "My brother just died, E.Z. I don't think any of 'em would begrudge me the need to get gone and clear my head for a few days."

Though neither one of them looked happy, E.Z. and Bear knew me well enough to know I'd made up my mind. We left things right there and I took my leave. Now there was only Mama Bear to convince. She respected me enough not to ask any questions, but I knew she'd suspect more going on than me needing a walkabout.

As I headed out to the lot, Shep got up to follow me. He caught me just as I climbed on my bike.

"You okay, man?" he asked, his eyes dark and grim. As Bear's son, I had a fleeting fear that maybe Bear had shared something about Beth with him. But he said nothing to indicate he knew anything about her.

"I just need a few days to clear my head. Don't worry about me."

Shep smiled. "We always worry about you, Deacon. Without you, the rest of us are fucked. Haven't you figured that out yet?" He meant it half-jokingly, but his words hung heavy around my neck. I knew they were true. The men in this club leaned on me. It was a mantle I felt comfortable carrying, but not today. So I turned it back on Shep.

"You want to tell me what's going on with you?" I asked. Shep's eyes darkened.

"Just want to make sure your head's good, that's all."

I smiled. "You know, lying's a sin." I was busting his balls, but something flickered behind Shep's eyes and I knew I'd hit a nerve.

"Just take care of yourself, man," he said, reaching out to shake my hand. "Like I said, we'd all be pretty well fucked without you."

I leaned forward, clasping Shep's fist; we bumped chests and I pulled my helmet on. If I hurried, I could pick up a few things from my house and be back in Crystal Falls before the sunset. I'd have to ditch the Harley and my cut if I had any hope of staying inconspicuous. As I left Shep and the clubhouse behind, my heart soared at the thought of being near Beth again. At the same time, I knew just how dangerous that could be for both of us.

Forgive me, Father, for I have sinned.

Chapter 6

Beth

When Darlene and Ed pressed me about who Danny was, I blew them off. What could I say? Ed might be a drunk, but he was also a brilliant man. On his worst days, he was still the best lawyer in town. The trouble was, his worst days were becoming his normal days and nothing Darlene or I said seemed to make any difference.

For my part, I tried to keep Danny/Deacon off my mind by cleaning up after Ed. We had three new divorce cases to file and custody motions early next week. I met with the clients, skirting the bounds of practicing law once again. I knew one day soon, Ed wouldn't be able to rest on the glory of his past reputation and goodwill of the local judiciary. If I wasn't careful, somebody was going to call us on it.

For now, Ed signed the pleadings I prepared and I took his word for it that he'd read them. Crystal Falls was stuck in the twentieth century on a lot of things. One of them was their court filing system. It would probably be another fifty years before they switched to electronic filing. So, I shlepped across town and gave everything to the clerk by hand.

I made it down exactly two of the courthouse steps before a deep voice shouted my name. "Beth!" I turned and shielded my eyes from the sun. Sheriff Beckett Finch came bounding up to me, his campaign hat in hand.

"Hey, Sheriff," I said, waving. My heart sank. Beckett had a grim look on his handsome face. Nearly five o'clock and the man was still cleanly shaven. He had a kind twinkle in his blue eyes but I knew there was something wrong.

"You got a minute?" he asked, gently touching my elbow. Beckett Finch was roughly my age. One of the youngest town sheriffs in the state, he'd come to Crystal Falls after I did under circumstances some thought just as strange. He, too, didn't like to talk about his past. In his case, most of his were public record. He'd been a Navy SEAL serving in the Middle East.

"Sure," I said, glancing behind me. I said a little prayer that whatever Ed had gotten himself into today, he wasn't hurt.

""Look," Beckett said. He ushered me to a shaded area beneath a tall elm in the town square. "I don't mean to pry into your business, but I just wanted to make sure everything was okay with you."

I did a double take. I didn't know whether to feel relief or indignation. Whatever this was, he wasn't here about Ed, it seemed.

"With me? Uh. Of course. I mean ... what have you heard?"

Beckett chewed his bottom lip. He had a deep cleft in his chin that lent him a rugged charm he wasn't even aware of. Whether he knew it or not, Beckett Finch, bachelor sheriff, was considered the catch of the county. To me, he'd just been a solid friend who didn't ask too many personal questions. Until now, apparently.

"Listen, this is a little awkward for me. And I'm the last one who wants to give credence or even much attention to gossip, but ... rumor has it you had an out-of-town visitor the other day."

My mouth ran dry. Of course. This was Crystal Falls. Danny probably hadn't made it off U.S. 10 before half the town saw him headed this way.

"Really?"

Beckett spun his hat in his hand. To his credit, the turn of this conversation seemed to make him just as miserable as it did me. On the one hand, his concern was sweet. On the other, I just wish everyone in this town would mind their own business.

"Are you going to make me come out and say it? Look, I heard you got manhandled by a member of the Dark Saints M.C. Is there something I should know about? Do you need anything?"

Manhandled? I rubbed my brow with my index finger. "No!" My answer came out more abrupt than I wanted. "No." I tried again, softer. "I mean, thank you for your concern, but it's not necessary. Whoever told you that was mistaken. That guy was just an … acquaintance. He brought me some news about somebody we both used to know."

What else could I say? I'd been so used to guarding my secrets, saying nothing that could clue anyone into where I was from or who I knew from before. Was it really safe now that Sean was dead? Danny had said a lot of things, but I still didn't know what to believe. Trust no one. That's how I'd lived my life for the last ten years. Beckett Finch was still part of that list, fair or not.

"Beth, are you sure? If there's someone harassing you, you know you can come to me. No questions asked."

"I know. And thank you. But honestly, there's no *there* there with this one."

Beckett didn't seem convinced. He creased his brow and slid his hat back on his head. "So this acquaintance, is he planning on making a repeat visit?"

Now he was Sheriff Finch again. Though it rankled me, I couldn't really blame him. It was his job to keep tabs on everything that happened in Crystal Falls. I knew he didn't want it to get overrun with an M.C. like Port Azrael. As it was, we were smack dab in the middle of territories run by the Devils Hawks out of Laredo, and the Saints in Port Az.

My heart skipped as I tried to think of an answer. Was Danny coming back? Did I want him to? I got a little woozy as I looked at Beckett. He read the conflict in my face and his expression fell. I forced a smile but it was too late. My poker face was slipping today. Danny had rattled me to my core.

"Just remember what I said, okay, Beth? If you need anything, you know how to get a hold of me."

"Thanks, Sheriff," I said, giving him a weak salute. "If you don't mind, I've got to head back to the office."

He nodded. "Me too, I guess. I'll see you around, Beth." Beckett shot me a good-natured wink and went on his way.

He was just doing his job. Beckett was one of the good guys. I knew all of this. Still, every alarm bell in me rang. For ten years, I'd built a wall around myself. I never got too close to anyone. Never trusted. Every new person I met, I wondered if it was someone Sean had sent to find me. Or worse ... one of his enemies. Now that he was ... dead ... I could barely allow myself to think it. It didn't seem real.

I went on auto-pilot the rest of the day, taking client statements for Ed, getting his reading material ready for tomorrow's hearings. Darlene swore she'd make him look at all of it. Normally, I'd stick around to make sure. Today, I just didn't have it in me. I just wanted a quiet night alone, to think.

I owned a little brick bungalow on Magnolia Street, a half a mile from downtown. It was quiet here, the name fit. Pink magnolia trees lined the sidewalk, casting shade during the hottest part of the day. The houses here were built right after

WWII, craftsman style, made for couples ready to start new families.

I had three bedrooms, a small kitchen, and dining area. A little porch off the back led to my fenced-in yard. For years, I'd been meaning to remodel, knock out the wall between the kitchen and living room and open up the floor plan like I'd seen done on every home-remodeling show on TV. Someday, maybe I'd get to it.

My furniture had been a hodgepodge of different styles, things I'd picked up at estate sales and discount stores. Even in my decorating, it seemed I couldn't commit anymore. The house was quiet and dark when I walked in. It's what I'd wanted, but now it just felt cold and empty. The weight of what Danny told me pressed on me here in the stillness.

I poured myself a glass of wine. Then another. Then a third. Halfway through it, my head spun and I felt the pressure in my chest ease. I did something I hadn't done in almost ten years. I went to the little wooden box I kept under my bed.

Heading back out into the living room, I set my wine on the table and opened the box. I didn't know why I kept these little trinkets, of all things. There were the keys to my parents' house in Port Azrael. I'm ashamed to say I didn't miss them. I'd grown up in turmoil with two raging alcoholics who took turns physically abusing each other. My mother died of liver failure when I was just nineteen years old, the year after I married Sean. Last I heard, my dad had hitchhiked to Canada chasing after yet another get-rich-quick scheme that would never pan out.

Sean was supposed to be my savior. Instead, he'd ended up my jailer. Still, the keys connected me to something that felt real at times when the ground shifted beneath me. I had a letter from my tenth-grade English teacher, Mrs. Watkins. She'd written me a glowing college recommendation. She was the first adult to truly believe in me. At the very bottom, I kept two framed pictures.

Smoothing away the dust, I picked up the first. It was Sean and me on the day we got married. We stood on the steps of the Port Az courthouse. Eighteen. I'd been just eighteen. The thirteen years since seemed like they could have been a hundred. Sean looked tan and healthy. He held me close, wrapping his arm around my small waist. I wore a pink suit that I'd stolen from my mother's closet. The sleeves were too long.

I'd loved him then. Sean had been my whole world. I was too young to see through the lies he told. The money came too easy. Flashy cars. Jewelry. He promised me the moon. I would have just settled for stability.

When I lifted the second picture, my heart twisted. It was the three of us. Sean, Danny, and me. We'd gone fishing off the pier. Sean had a trout on the line and swung it toward me, taunting me. He was laughing, but there was a glint in his eye that cut through me. This was later, just a few months before everything turned to dust. Danny stood in the background, leaning against his truck, watching. The smile on his face didn't reach his eyes. Those were glued to me.

I pressed the picture frame to my chest. Danny held a secret in his eyes. His sin. It should have been my shame. But even now, after so much time had passed, the memory of what we shared still flickered as a tiny flame inside my heart. If I tended to it, that flame would grow. How many nights had I let it engulf me, leaving me gasping for air and my sex thrumming with the echoes of pleasure?

"Damn you, Sean," I whispered. "Everything you touched turned to dust."

The wine played a part, I'm sure. Opening the box had been a bad idea as my emotions churned and overtook me. God help me, I missed Sean. Not the man he turned into or revealed himself to be. He'd been cruel, sadistic, dangerous. But the man I thought I'd married. And I missed Danny too at the same time I cursed him for leaving me all alone.

I don't remember doing it. But before I knew what was happening, I threw the wooden box against the wall. It felt good. Cathartic. I grabbed the picture frame and hurled it as hard as I could. The glass shattered into a million pieces. I felt foolish for a second, but then relief flooded through me. Tears streamed down my face. I picked up the wedding photo and threw that too. It ricocheted, hitting the end table beside me. Glass flew up and stung the corner of my eye.

"Shit!" I yelled. I had a large mirror hanging on the opposite wall. I got a little dizzy as I stood and saw a trickle of blood running down my cheek.

"Great," I muttered, staggering toward the kitchen. I only made it three steps before the front door burst open and Deacon Wade loomed in front of me, his eyes cold as steel.

Chapter 7

Deacon

I scanned the room, reaching for the 9mm I kept holstered at my side. I'd heard breaking glass and Beth's shout. The rest was a blur. She held her fingers to her forehead; blood trickled down the side of her face. Her eyes wide with terror, she stumbled back toward the kitchen.

"Beth?" I reached for her. There were shards of glass all over the living room but she was alone. She looked at me wide-eyed, incredulous.

"Where did you come from?" she asked, slurring her words a little. Then the clarity of the situation sank in. There was no danger. No intruder. I saw an empty wine glass sat on an end table with a tan lipstick mark on the rim. Two shattered picture frames lay upside down on the floor. I don't know why it mattered, but I leaned down and picked one up. My heart twisted when I saw the torn picture inside. It was Beth.

Sean and Beth. I'd been the one to snap it on the courthouse steps the day he married her. I'd stood up for both of them. Sean's best man and Beth's man of honor. I let the picture fall to the ground and went to her.

"Let's get you cleaned up," I said, gently taking her by the arm. Beth's eyes went up and up. She blinked hard as if she was trying to convince herself she wasn't dreaming me. Hell, I was doing a little of the same. My heart thundered inside me as the blood poured from the cut on her temple. It wasn't deep, but she'd likely nicked a capillary or something.

She let me lead her into her small kitchen. The place reminded me a little of my parents' house. Mid-century modern with long, narrow countertops and a door leading to the back porch. Simple. Quiet. I couldn't help looking for little cues that might tell me whether Beth lived alone.

I put my hands on her waist and lifted her to the countertop. Her breath hitched as her feet left the ground. I let my hands linger for a moment, loving the feel of her in my arms. Then I got a hold of myself and grabbed a towel she had neatly folded by the sink. I let the cold water run over it and pressed it to the little gash above her left eye.

"What are you doing here?" she asked, hissing from the sting of the cloth.

"You always leave your front door unlocked like that?" I asked. My pulse hadn't quieted. Her scream. The glass. I squeezed my eyes shut and got a hold of myself.

"I wasn't ... I didn't ..." She let out a defeated sigh and took the cloth from me. She waved me off when I tried to help her down.

"You always come barging in unannounced?" she asked, the fire back in her eyes. I can't help that it churned something inside of me. Dammit. What the hell had I been thinking? I was just supposed to keep an eye on her. I wasn't supposed to get in her life again.

"I heard you scream," I said. "I thought ..."

She pulled the cloth away from her eye. My protective instincts fueled me and I pulled her into the light. "Do you have a first-aid kit somewhere?" The bleeding had stopped but she needed antiseptic and something to close the wound.

"Under the sink," she said, defeated. I didn't wait for permission. I pulled out the little red box she kept and rummaged through it until I found some antibiotic cream and butterfly strips.

"Keep still," I said.

Beth backed up to the counter. I towered over her, feeling her hot breath against my neck. Her eyes darted back and forth as I dotted her cut with the medicine and carefully applied the butterfly strips.

"That should do it," I said. "It should heal without a scar if you keep it clean."

"Hmm. Since when did you take up the practice of medicine?" I knew she meant it as a joke, but the smile died on her lips when she saw my expression. The truth was, running with the Dark Saints had brought me my share of near misses. I'd learned a thing or two at Mama Bear's side. She'd been an army medic in her day. It came in handy more than once over the years as she patched up the membership after whatever scrape we got in.

"What are you *doing* here, Danny?" she asked.

I froze. I didn't want to lie to her. I'd promised her the other day that she was safe. How in the hell could I stick to that if I told her the truth? I was worried about her. Until we knew for sure who capped Sean and why, she wasn't completely free. I'd only been back in her life a few days and already the lying had started.

She knew it too.

"You're checking up on me," she said. She placed her hands behind her, gripping the countertop. I still stood close, holding the bandage wrappers in my hand. In that tight little kitchen, I felt sure she could hear my heart pumping.

It had been ten years, but I could still remember the taste of her. I could still hear the little gasps of pleasure she made when she spread herself open for me. Lust made it hard to see. My hands trembled and I finally broke away, busying myself with the damn first-aid kit.

"What aren't you telling me?" Beth asked. She put a hand on my arm, pulling me back to look at her. "Danny ... Deacon ... please."

It got hard to breathe. Why in the hell had I thought I could be close to her again without feeling the same aching temptation? I'd been stupid enough to think the years would have dulled it. Now I knew they hadn't. If anything, I burned even hotter for her.

I forced myself to think of Sean. Not as he was, but what I saw in the morgue. But when I closed my eyes, a horror flashed behind them. It wasn't Sean I saw on that slab, but Beth. My eyes snapped open and a monster roared inside of me.

I took her by the shoulders. Beth gasped. My pulse thundered in my temples. I wanted. I needed.

"It's okay," I said, my voice raw. "At least, it's *probably* okay. I just wanted to make sure you were good. That's all."

"You know something you're not telling me," she said. "Nothing's changed. Not one single thing."

She went someplace in her mind. Whatever was happening to me, something similar took over Beth. Sense memories are the strongest. At least, that's what they always say. Her scent, her touch. She was talking about something else, but every word she'd just said was true. Nothing had changed. Not one single thing.

She reached for me, touching a light hand to my cheek. It sent electric fire arcing through me. This was Beth. This was me and Beth. Ten years evaporated in a heartbeat. Adrenaline and desire fueled me. The truth was, it hadn't stopped since the moment I saw her the other day. My fear for her ignited something primal, something I'd tried to bury for so long.

And it caught fire in her too. I saw the flame behind her eyes.

Beth's breath came up short. Her hands slid up my chest. It was new and familiar all at once.

"Danny," she whispered. For the first time in a long time, the name felt like it belonged to me. No. It belonged to her.

She trembled against me. Her eyes glistened as they darted over me. Her lips parted. They were soft and sweet; a hint of a blush colored her cheeks. She wore a thin t-shirt cut into a low vee. I took in every detail. The swell of her breasts tempted me. I wanted to run my tongue along the cleft between them, tasting every inch of her.

I leaned down, desire swirling between us. Time stopped. We were nowhere. I brought my lips to hers and a moan rumbled out of me. Beth leaned into the kiss, swaying on her feet. I wrapped one arm around her waist and pressed her against me. I felt a new, delicious curve to her hips. God, I wanted to explore every inch of her and see what else had changed. I was more afraid of what might have stayed the same.

I could taste berries on her lips. It was the wine she drank and it seemed to ignite my blood right along with hers. Down and down I went, pulled by my need for her.

Beth. *My* Beth. Ten years ago I'd taken what didn't belong to me and it ripped our worlds apart. I wanted to do it all over again.

Beth swayed on her feet and my head swirled. I don't know what reached me in that heady fog of desire. No. That's not true. I knew what it was, I just couldn't bring myself to name it.

Damn my honor. I wanted to sin.

When she whispered my name, it brought me back into myself. Beth staggered sideways, bringing the back of her hand to her swollen lips.

"Beth," I said, gasping. "Dammit." I stepped away from her, tearing my hand through my hair. She didn't deserve this. She deserved better than me. And yet, here I was, trying to claim something that wasn't mine to take.

"I'm sorry," I said. "I shouldn't ..."

"No ..." she said, stepping around me. She reached for a glass and poured herself water from the tap. I loved watching the column of her throat work as she swallowed. I still loved everything about her. She steadied herself against the counter and carefully set the glass down.

"You got a dustpan and a broom somewhere?" I asked. "Let me take care of that mess in the living room."

She turned toward me but I didn't give her a chance to answer. I guessed right. A little door off the kitchen led to a utility closet and I quickly found what I needed. Beth stood dumbstruck as I went into the living room and swept up the broken glass. I was fast and efficient, trying to sweep away the broken pieces of my heart as if it were the glass.

Beth collected herself and opened the cabinet under the sink, pointing me to the trash can. "You still haven't told me why you're really here, Deacon."

Deacon. I was Deacon again. It was for the best. I'd brought this woman nothing but heartache and ruin since the moment she met me. And she brought me ... No. I couldn't bring myself to think it.

"It's club business, Beth. That's all I can really say."

She clapped her hands together in a sweeping gesture. "Right. That's your party line now, is it? I think I already know the rest of the words to this song. I should just trust you, is that it?"

I let out a hard breath and leaned against the counter. Beth stepped around me and took a seat at her kitchen table. Color had come back into her cheeks. She was more sober than she had been a few minutes ago. With clarity came her anger. I knew I deserved it.

"This is almost over," I said. "I can tell you that much. And I know I should have probably waited to come here. But Sean's murder has been in the news. It's local only, but I knew there was a pretty good chance it would reach you. I knew you'd have questions so I figured I owed it to you to ..."

"Owed me?" Fire flashed behind Beth's eyes. I recognized it as a little of the alcohol still fueling her, but the rest was legit fury. "Owed me? Jesus, Danny, you sound like your brother. He had a gift for turning my anger back on me and making me feel like *I* was the one doing something wrong."

"No," I said. "You've never done anything wrong, Beth. Not you. I didn't mean that. There are only so many times I can tell you I'm sorry. You don't deserve any of this. You think I don't know what you've sacrificed? But yeah, I'm asking you to trust me. I'm asking you to sit tight for just a little while longer until I'm sure none of this can touch you."

She blanched. "Touch me," she whispered, and her unshed tears glistened in her eyes again.

And once again, I'd done everything wrong where this woman was concerned. Every time I walked into her life, I left carnage in my wake.

"You Wade brothers have a real knack for touching me, Danny," she said, her voice taking a faraway quality.

"Beth, listen."

She put a hand up. This time, she let the tears fall. I felt each one like a knife in my gut. "You should go," she said. "Crystal Falls is a small town. You can't be here."

I knew what she meant. I'd drawn stares when I rode through the other day. This time, I'd tried to be more inconspicuous, at least. I'd left the Harley in Port Az and worn civilian clothes. Just a t-shirt and worn jeans.

"Will you just be careful and lay low for the next couple of days?" I asked. "Do you have any vacation time coming to you?"

"You want me to hide?" she asked. "Is it that serious?"

"No," I said quickly, not wanting to scare her any more than I already had.

"Right," she said. "Trust you. Well, Deacon, the answer is no. I'm not going to take any vacation days. I can't afford them.

You said yourself, nobody besides you knows I'm even here. I appreciate the extra effort, but I can take care of myself. I've been doing it long enough."

Something flickered behind her eyes. She'd put up her shields and I was glad of it. I stood in her kitchen for a moment, searching for the thing I could say that would take the hurt out of her eyes. Then I knew there was nothing.

"I should go," I said. Beth closed her eyes slowly and nodded.

"Take care of yourself, Danny," she said, pressing her fingers to her lips. As I walked out her front door, I could still taste her and my heart churned with a mix of desire and regret. Once again, I'd hurt the only person I ever truly loved.

Chapter 8

Deacon

Beth's touch lingered on my lips. The desire I felt for her hadn't dampened one bit in the last ten years. If anything, it had grown more intense. But she was vulnerable; no matter what else he was, my brother had been her husband. She'd built her life waiting for some other shoe to drop with him. We both had. First, it had been the flashy cars and expensive trips he wanted to take her on. Sean had a respectable job as a sanitation worker, but it wasn't enough to afford the fast cars and diamonds he brought her.

Then, Sean had started bringing people to the house that scared Beth. She'd been afraid to confide in me at first. But in my line of work, I knew every corner of Port Azrael and I recognized members of one of the most dangerous drug cartels when I saw them. Sean made all the promises guys like him usually make. They were just friends. He wasn't involved in their businesses. Finally, Sean started disappearing for weeks at a time and Beth got followed home.

I remember that first night like it was yesterday. I found her in the last pew at San Mateo's. She'd been waiting for me. She didn't want to betray my brother, but she was worried about him. Then she was worried about herself. We worked out a system. She came to church twice a week and sat in that back pew. If she missed a day, I knew something was wrong.

I used to tell myself that she needed me and I had to be there for her. It was my vocation, after all. Though she was my sister-in-law, she was also a parishioner. But after a while, it became something else. I needed her. I was the one who was weak. When she cried on my shoulder, I felt the supple outlines of her body. I grew drunk with the scent of her perfume. And each week, the things Sean did grew worse. She'd recorded his conversations, documented the calls he received and where he went. There was no mistake. Sean was moving up the ranks as a major dealer for the cartel.

Then Beth wanted out. One terrible night, she confronted Sean. I had no idea she was planning it. Sean beat her within an inch of her life. Too scared to go back, I got her into the small convent associated with San Mateo's and we met in the gardens every single day as the sisters nursed Beth back to health.

I was thinking of Beth sitting on the stone bench in front of the rose bushes. That's where she'd always wait for me. Alone. Pale. Scared. But a fire flickered in her eyes when she saw me. That fire still burned; it flared to life when she kissed me tonight.

When I pulled into the clubhouse lot, I got the first sense that something wasn't right. Mama usually waited in the doorway when one of us had taken off for a few days. The woman knew how unsettled I was. I think she also knew it wasn't completely about Sean.

When I came into the main room, Mama was treating Shep at the bar. Blood ran in rivers down his chest and he hissed as she worked a needle through his shoulder.

"What the hell's going on?" I asked. It looked like a battlefield hospital in here. I realized with horror that's exactly what this was. Mama was almost done with Shep, but Axle lay on the table in the back of the room, his arm heavily bandaged.

Bear stormed out of the conference room. He was on his burner phone shouting orders to some of the other guys. "You tell everybody in Abilene to lay low. You get Chase, Toby, and Zig to the safehouse there."

"Here!" Mama barked at me. She tossed me a packet of disinfectant soap. "Scrub up in the sink. I'm going to need you to hold him down while I finish these stitches. Bullet passed straight through."

"Bullet? What the hell's going on?"

"Ambush, that's what!" E.Z. roared as he came out of the conference room behind Bear. "Axle and Shep were making a gun drop up the coast. Cops were waiting in the weeds. Somebody tipped 'em off."

"Cops shot you?" I finished scrubbing up in the sink and put on a pair of purple latex gloves so I could assist Mama. Shep looked gray, but he was sitting upright. Mama's face was hard and determined, but she wasn't panicking. Her son's wound wasn't deep. It looked like the bullet had just grazed the fleshy part of Shep's shoulder. A little more to the left and it could have shredded major arteries or done serious muscle damage. By the looks of it, he'd just have an ugly scar. Shep bore his mother's treatment with a stony face.

"Yeah," Shep said. "It was a rookie deputy. Got trigger happy. He was a lousy fucking shot."

"Lucky for you!" Mama scolded.

"Just one?" I asked. It didn't make any sense. If the cops had been tipped off we were making a drop, why wasn't the A.T.F. on it?

"He was in the right place at the right time," Shep answered, flinching as Mama debrided his wound. She took the needle from me. I put my hands on Shep's shoulders and held him steady as she closed the edges of his wound.

"Axle too?" I asked.

"Nah," Axle shouted from his position on the table. "Just got a little banged up trying to run interference and grab Shep. Nothing worse than a little road burn."

"Well," Mama said. "I've done about all I can do here." She snapped her gloves off and put a gentle hand on her son's back. She looked scared. I don't think I'd ever seen her like that. Shep reached up and touched the back of her head, pulling her forward so he could kiss her.

"I'm okay, Mama. Go on home. Bear's going to want to talk."

She glared at her husband over Shep's head. He was still on the phone but gave her a nod. It did nothing to placate her but Mama Bear knew the drill. I told her I'd clean up the mess. She grabbed her purse and stormed out of the clubhouse. Bear would have hell to pay with her later.

Bear snapped his burner phone shut. We were on a skeleton crew here at the house. Shep and Axle were handling the drop up the coast. The main action was taking place in Abilene. I should have been with them. Bear wouldn't say it, but I knew he had to be thinking it.

As soon as he was sure Mama got in her car and drove off, he ran a hard hand over his face. "It's bad," he said.

"Did we lose anybody today?" I asked, my heart turning to ash.

"No, thank God," Bear said. "But it was damn close. And this was too fucking coordinated. Somebody knew the crews were gonna be split today."

"This is the Hawks!" E.Z.'s booming voice rattled the hanging beer mugs. Axle hauled himself off the back table and went to stand by Shep. I still had that weird vibe from the both of them. They knew something. Whatever it was, they weren't saying it in front of Bear or E.Z. That couldn't be good.

"I just got off with Chase," Bear said. "Our suppliers in Abilene are pulling out. We aren't going to make the shipment with our friends up north. It's a fucking house of cards and it all just folded."

"You think this little mishap with Axle and Shep was connected?" I asked.

"I think Galveston County deputies got the okay to rattle our guys. That's new. And it's not good. It was a warning shot. But it might not have been from an obvious source."

"What do you mean?" Shep asked. His color was a little better now. He disregarded his mother's orders and poured himself a shot of bourbon. I couldn't blame him.

"I mean if the Hawks had enough rope to hang us, they'd have called the A.T.F., not those Barney Fife locals. You remember we heard about a hotshot new agent out of their field office wanting to make a name for himself? What's his name? Wright? White? Anyway, I think this was just somebody's way of letting us know they *could* have done worse if they wanted to."

"Somebody." E.Z. paced the length of the bar. "This ain't a mystery, Bear."

"Look," Bear said, "We need everybody in one place. But right now, I need the others in Abilene to lay low. If Shep and Axle got ambushed, we gotta watch our asses for the next day or two. I wanna figure out just who tipped off that deputy. He could be working for the Hawks too. I don't know how deep this goes. But yeah, this is coming to a vote sooner rather than later."

My heart sank. For Bear to even say that meant the outcome was certain. He'd tried to hold the line as long as he could, but war was coming for the Dark Saints. From the looks of things, it was coming from all sides.

"E.Z., you're with me," Bear said. "We're riding up the coast. Chase is going to meet us halfway. You three sit tight here at the clubhouse. Stay out of sight until you hear from me."

I didn't like the idea of Bear riding out in the open with just E.Z. to watch his six, but he'd made up his mind. Once he had, they moved quickly. I cleaned up the bloodied bandages and straightened the bar. When the front door closed, it was Axle, me, and Shep.

"Where you been, man?" Shep wasted no time getting into my business. I realized with growing horror what it might look like to him. And it would have been *my* job to ride with Shep and Axle today if Bear hadn't let me look after Beth in Crystal Falls. Would it have made a difference?

"I've had some ... family shit to take care of."

A look passed between Shep and Axle. It was the same one I'd seen from them for weeks now.

"You want to clue me in on what's going on? I know you guys. You're acting cagey, like you know something. And you're not bringing it to Bear. You gonna clue me in?"

"Everybody's just antsy," Axle said, trying to shut me down. "With good reason. Bear's right about one thing. It was too much of a damn coincidence today. At the exact same time Shep and I get jumped, Chase and the others have hell breaking loose in Abilene. Somebody knew where we were going to be and coordinated this shit today."

"You think it was me?" I couldn't keep the anger out of my voice. I knew I wasn't misreading the looks on their faces. I waited for one of them to point out that I was the only one AWOL during everything today.

"Calm your shit," Axle said. "Nobody's saying that. It's just, everybody needs to stick close for the time being, is all. Divided, we could get conquered."

"I told you," I said. "I had some family business to deal with out of town."

"Listen," Shep said. "We've all got to sort out our family business. That's what Bear was telling Chase on the phone before you walked in."

"What do you mean?" A cold chill ran through my heart. I knew exactly what he meant. If the Hawks had declared war already, it looked more and more like Sean's murder was the opening shot. And it meant they were going after people close to us.

I felt sick to my stomach. In my attempt to keep Beth safe, had I unwittingly led danger right to her doorstep?

"I gotta go," I said.

"Deacon, you can't." Axle put a vice-like grip on my shoulder. I jerked away. He was still a little woozy from his scrape-up. Any other day, he wouldn't have let go.

"I've got no choice," I said. "You tell me ... and I mean really tell me. Has Bear put the word out to circle the wagons? Is he worried about your wives and families?"

Axle looked down and it was all the answer I needed.

"Shit," I said under my breath. How stupid could I be? I'd ridden into Crystal Falls the other day in my cut. People had seen Beth with me. I thought Sean was the biggest danger to her. I'd been so wrong. The danger to Beth was me.

Chapter 9

Beth

Edward Albright, Esquire had a run of a few good days. But only a few. He managed to talk his way out of any sanctions by Judge Dupree over missing his motion hearing earlier in the month, but everyone knew he'd likely used the absolute last drop of goodwill he had in this town. But I also knew he hadn't yet hit rock bottom. It seemed I had a knack for attracting lost causes. Even now.

I tried to put it out of my mind, but I felt Danny everywhere. For ten years I'd tried to tell myself that what we had was just the product of pain and desperate circumstances. It was. But seeing him again ... *feeling* him had my heart spinning. If I could have just buried myself in my work, that would have been okay. But with Eddie firmly off the wagon, the work was starting to dry up.

ical stare of hers. There was nothing to do but keep that smile in place as I turned and watched the front door open.

Danny was so tall, the top of his head nearly brushed the doorframe. He wore his leather cut again with those weathered jeans and motorcycle boots. For the first time since he'd sauntered back into my life, I realized it suited him. Or at least, he wore it more comfortably than the cassock I'd been so used to seeing him in a hundred years ago.

"Back conference room's open," Darlene said, smiling. I'm not sure if she meant that for my benefit or Danny's. *Every* other room in the office was open. Ed hadn't actually come in for three days.

Danny stood frozen, those piercing blue eyes cutting straight through me. "I'm sorry to just drop in on you like this. Ma'am?" He dipped his chin toward Darlene, smiling; she let out a swooning little sigh and rested her chin on her palm. She *had* been watching too many soap operas.

There was no way I would take Danny to the conference room or anywhere else in the building. The walls were too thin and Darlene was like a dog with a bone.

"Do you have a minute?" Danny asked, clearing his throat. I reached over Darlene's desk and grabbed my small purse. I slung it over my shoulder and shot her a quick smile.

"Seeing as Ed's probably not going to grace us with his presence today, I'm going to take an early lunch. I'll be back within the hour."

I put on a brave face for Darlene. She'd read enough into

everything. Danny made another polite apology then followed me out the front door. I knew damn well Darlene would watch everything from her monitor. At least there was no sound.

"My truck's in the shop," I said. "I took a cab to work. We can't talk here though."

I couldn't believe I was actually suggesting this, but it seemed I had no choice. Danny gave me a slow nod and walked down the porch steps with me. There was nothing left to do but climb on the back of his Harley.

My hands trembled as I slid them around Deacon's waist. Deacon. In that moment as he revved his engine and slid into the seat, that's who he became. The bike felt like an extension of his body. Power. Sleek control. Total freedom. I understood instantly why he took to it.

My hair whipped behind me as we picked up speed, heading toward the highway. Deacon took the curves with expert ease. He knew exactly where he was going. I envied that about him. In a lot of ways, I'd been so unsure of things over the last ten years. I'd left everything I knew behind to start a new life. I'd done it so I could feel safe and free. I realized Danny had done the very same thing and this bike and the patch he wore were part of it. A part of me resented him a little bit for it.

He rode out to the desert just past Crystal Falls, finding the turn-off to Devil's Hole. It was an ominous location. In the middle of nowhere under the shade of a few tall red cedar trees, three flat stones formed a semi-circle around a hole in the ground. Legend had it the hole was so deep, no one had ever been able to accurately measure it. The locals said the place was haunted by the ghosts of union sympathizers from the Civil War and Reconstruction. Those men allegedly met their fate somewhere in that bottomless pit.

Danny cut his engine and climbed off first. Then he held his hand out to me and we walked to the stone benches together.

This place. This man. Everything came flooding back to me. I'd met my fate with Danny "Deacon" Wade ten years ago on a stone bench not that different from this one. Before, we found each other before a reflecting pool behind the San Mateo church rectory. A towering statue of the Virgin Mary witnessed our sins. This time, we met before the ghosts of long-forgotten soldiers.

"What is it?" I finally said.

Danny rubbed his palm with the thumb of the opposite hand. Everything had changed, and yet nothing had. He used to do the same thing so many years ago when there was something troubling him. And I did the same thing I used to do. I reached for him, bringing his hands into my lap. My touch jolted him. We fell into old patterns so quickly.

"I have reason to think Sean's murder had more to do with my club than it did his ... associations."

I peered into his face. "What are you talking about?"

Danny looked up at me. The urge to touch his face burned through me. I wanted to take the pain from his eyes. "My club," he said. "Things are unsettled between us and the Devils Hawks. You remember who they are?"

Nodding, I slowly closed my eyes. You couldn't grow up in Port Azrael without knowing full well who the Dark Saints and Devils Hawks M.C. were. As rough a reputation as the Saints had, I also knew they kept even worse elements out of Port Az. The Hawks were about as bad an element as there was.

"You think Sean was mixed up with a rival M.C.?"

Danny shrugged. "Probably not directly. And I can't get too specific, but we have reason to believe what happened to Sean was a message."

"What kind of message?"

Danny turned to me. He kept his cool, but a tiny flickering vein near his temple clued me in how worried he really was. "Enough people knew Sean was my brother. It's possible killing him was a way to let the rest of us know the Hawks are changing the rules."

"What rules?" My throat ran dry. I couldn't sit still. I stood up and started to pace. No. No. No. It was the same. We'd had the exact same conversation ten years ago when Danny told me Sean was messed up with the cartel. No one around Sean had been safe after that.

"We don't touch families," Danny said. He was talking into space, his expression hard. I knew him. After all these years, I still knew him. And after all these years I still felt his pain as my own. I sank back to the stone beside him.

"You think somebody killed Sean to get to you?" I didn't know how to even feel about it. Grief? In all the ways that mattered, I'd buried Sean Wade and the life I had with him years ago.

The wind kicked up, rustling Danny's hair. I acted without thinking, raising my hand to smooth it back. Danny flinched. It was an old, familiar gesture. It was who we were before on that bench not so different from this one. Only then, the rain had started. If I closed my eyes, I could see him; I could put myself right back there. I heard the words he spoke, raw and hard.

He's dead. Oh, God. Beth. He's dead.

I saw Danny as he was that night, pale, tortured. All the prayers we'd shared together came to nothing. We couldn't save Sean. We couldn't save each other. And Danny's worst fear had come true. Sean's demons had reached out and stolen their father from them. The cartel had come to our house one night. I'd been gone. I'd come to the garden to be with Danny.

"No," I whispered. "Sean's dead because his life finally caught up with him. We always knew it would end like this for him."

"I wished they'd killed him that night," Danny whispered. He was right back there just like I was. We'd both spent a lifetime thinking about the what-ifs.

"He was too valuable to them," I said. "They weren't done using him."

I watched the color drain from Danny's face. If I closed my eyes, I could see the blood on his hands. His father's blood. They'd shot him in the chest in my living room. If I'd been there that night instead of with Danny, they would have shot me too.

"Don't," I said. "Don't do this. Don't blame yourself for living. Isn't that what you told me? We both think if we'd have done something different, maybe Sean would have listened. That more words spoken better could have saved him. Well, they couldn't. Sean made his choices. Maybe he loved us both once, but then it changed. It's taken me so long to come to grips with that. But I'm not to blame for what happened. Neither are you."

Danny went as rigid as the stone we sat on. God help me, more old patterns rose to the surface. I slid my arm around his shoulder and pressed my fingers to his chin, turning him toward me.

I was here. I was there, ten years ago. My head swam. If I closed my eyes, I could see Danny as he was standing over his father's casket. He became something different that day. A piece of his heart turned black. I remember Father Sanchez trying to reach him and knowing I was the only one who could. I alone knew his heart. Because he'd given it to me.

"Why did you leave, Danny?" I whispered, hating the pain in my voice. I knew he might hear it as "Why did you leave me?"; I meant that too, but not really.

"I had to keep you safe," he said and for a moment, I don't think he was talking to me.

"But I was safe," I said. "I don't regret coming to Crystal Falls.

I built a life for myself here. I have friends. I have a job that I like."

"Do you?" he asked. "Come on, Beth. I've seen enough to know this isn't what you really want. You were going to go to law school. You had to give that up because of Sean's mess."

"I don't have any regrets. There's no point to it. You shouldn't either."

"Shouldn't I?" Danny's voice took a hard edge that sounded just like Sean's. It set me off. I reacted out of disproportionate anger. Our emotions were both running so high.

"Don't tell me you left the church for me," I said, dropping his chin. "Don't you dare tell me that."

Silence thick as a wall rose between us. I knew I was picking at a wound that hadn't fully healed. It's the one thing that didn't make sense. Danny had a path. A calling. Even with Sean's drama, it made no sense for him to just leave it all behind. I couldn't bear it. I would *not* wear the shame of Danny's misplaced guilt.

"That's what you told them, isn't it?" I said, my voice full of accusation. "Father Sanchez? Did you think sleeping with me made you irredeemable?"

"Sleeping with you?"

"So that's it," I said, rising slowly. "You look at me and you see your greatest weakness. Your worst sin." Even as I tried to hurt him with my words, desire swelled within me. If I was

Danny's greatest sin, then he was mine. We took comfort from each other in that garden in the pelting rain under the statue of the Virgin Mary. It was the single most erotic moment of my life. I had plenty of regrets, but God help me, not that.

"No," Danny said, rising to meet me. He caught my wrists when I would have turned away from him. "I told you before. You weren't my greatest sin, Beth. You don't even make the top ten."

I wrenched my hand away and slapped him. Fire roared within me. Danny didn't so much as flinch. He took a steadying breath and caught my wrist again.

"That's not what I mean," he said.

I wanted to pull away. I wanted him to draw me closer. Pain, desire, rage, lust. It all swirled in my heart and took my breath from me.

"We should go," he said. "Let me take you back home."

"No!" I shouted. "Say what you came to say. You've been dancing around it."

"Beth ..."

"Tell me! What is it?"

He dropped his shoulders and then my wrists. I staggered backward, afraid to get any closer to him.

"I didn't leave the church because of you," he said, with a deep, flat tone that scared me a little. "And I didn't leave *for* you. And no, when I go to hell, fucking my brother's wife will be the least of the sins tallied against me."

"What was it? What happened to you, Danny? Tell me!"

A tremor went through him. He slowly lifted his eyes to mine and my heart stopped. I wanted to know but I didn't want to hear it.

"The cartel was going to kill you. They would have killed me too. And they killed my father. Sean was never going to make it right so I had to find a way to protect you. To protect my mother. I had to give them a reason to think twice about coming after any of us. So I had to find what I thought was an even bigger monster."

I took a staggering step backward. "The Dark Saints. You went to them for protection?"

Danny slowly nodded. My mouth dropped. "They made you join them? They made you give up your calling in exchange for what?"

"No," he whispered. "It wasn't like that. They never made me do anything. Everything that happened ... I asked for it, Beth. These men, my brothers ... they're my family now. But the cartel understands only one thing. Force for force. You didn't see him. You don't know."

I shook my head. Again, if I closed my eyes I could see the blood on his hands. "Danny?"

His eyes snapped open. "Deacon. My name is Deacon. And the Dark Saints gave me the one thing I couldn't get anywhere else. They filled something in me I never knew was missing. They allowed me vengeance. The men that came to your house that night? They'll never hurt you. They can't because they're dead. I killed them. With the fire and fury of the club behind me, I made them pay."

His greatest sin. My mouth dropped. Oh God. Oh Danny. He hadn't just become a dark saint. He had become an avenging angel.

Chapter 10

Deacon

She asked me to take her home as the sun began to set. Riding through that desert highway with Beth's arms wrapped around my waist was the closest thing to heaven I was likely to get. Now she knew why.

Thou shall not covet. I broke that vow the first time I laid eyes on Beth.

Thou shall not kill. My father's killers died at my hands. With the club backing me up, I'd ended the cartel's hitman. Bear wasn't stupid. I solved a problem for him too. He used me to send a message to the cartel and for a while, they pulled out of Port Azrael.

Thou shall not commit adultery. My dick still tightened at the memory of Beth's body pressed against mine. I wanted her then. I wanted her still.

I had broken nearly every other commandment. I'd broken every vow I made or meant to make to the church. I may have lost my soul, but I found myself in the process. My club. These men. I belonged. That's the secret I'd tried to keep for all these years. I didn't leave the church. I found my home.

"Come inside, Deacon," Beth said. The setting sun blazed an orange trail across the sky. Far in the distance, storm clouds rumbled.

"Beth. I came here because ... I'm trying to tell you that it may not be safe for you again. At least, not for a little while. Not because of Sean, because of me. I tried to do the right thing. But I think coming here was a mistake. If they find out ... if my enemies know what you mean to me ..."

She stood on her porch looking up at me. The fading sun made flecks of gold dance in her eyes. Ten years ago, she'd come to me for confession, absolution. We found it in each other with our bodies and souls. Now I came to her for the same thing.

Beth reached for me. She took my hands in hers and led me inside. I should have turned and left. I should have called Bear and put a couple of the probies on her house and her office. Just like before, there were a million things I should have done, but only one I did.

"Why *did* you come here?" she whispered, looking up at me. My eyes took in every detail of her then settled on the tiny pulse in her throat.

Her question cut me to the core. There were all the logical

answers I told myself. Because Beth deserved to hear about Sean from me. Because I needed to know that she was truly okay. Because things could get stirred up again and people connected to me needed protection. It was all true. And it was all a damn lie.

Thou shall not covet.

I don't know who moved first. Maybe we moved together. But Beth was in my arms. Her breasts pressed against the soft leather of my jacket. My lips were on her, setting off a firestorm inside me.

Fuck. It was over for me the minute I saw her and I was a damn fool to have thought otherwise.

We stumbled together until I had her backed up against the wall. I pulled her shirt out of her pants and slid my fingers up her ribcage, loving the trail of gooseflesh I made.

Her hands were on me too, peeling away my cut. I flipped off my t-shirt and Beth let out a little gasp. Her eyes registered an instant of shock, then a new flare of desire more heated than before. The years had changed me. My muscles were harder. She explored me with her fingers, finding the lines of ink over my chest and arms. There were battle scars too. You can't ride with the Dark Saints without spilling blood. Beth took it all in and kissed a path up my chest.

Then it was my turn to see her. She bit her bottom lip as I spread open her blouse. She wore a lacy pink bra that barely held her in. Her curves had rounded out in ways that revved me hard. I two-fingered the little clasp in front and her nipples spilled out.

Beth became my altar, just like she had ten years ago. I worshipped her, dropping to my knees as I kissed my way down. She threaded her fingers through my hair as I dragged her pants past her waist. She wore pretty little lace panties that matched the bra. I hooked my fingers beneath the waistband. Beth threw her head back as I pulled them down.

God. She spread for me like a ripe peach. I tasted her. Beth's knees trembled and I slid my hands between her thighs, pulling her wider apart. I flicked the tiny little bud between her legs and loved the way she quivered. Then I fastened my lips around her. I wanted this. I wanted her. I would make her come for me the first time as she writhed against the wall.

"Danny!" she cried out as the first waves of pleasure rocked her. She came so fast it startled me. My Beth. My sweet Beth. She was a little awkward, bucking against the wall. I wanted to believe it was because she'd waited all this time for me. Maybe it was, but it wasn't my right to expect it.

As she crested down, I turned her. Slowly, I guided her to the floor. Beth moved to kick off her heels.

"No," I whispered, my voice a wicked growl. "Leave those on." She looked so damn sexy like that, letting me dominate her.

Beth's breath hitched, but she did as I commanded. She went on all fours as I stroked myself. Oh God. She looked so good, it had to be a sin. But I didn't care. Beth was ready for me again, gaping. I swiped a finger between her legs and found her soaked.

She leaned down, practically pressing her chin to her hands. I couldn't help it, I wanted to take it all in. My Beth. My sweet Beth. I would claim her just like I had before. She was mine. She would always be mine even if it meant we were both damned to hell.

"Danny!" she whispered. Then something changed. I put a hand on her ass, giving her a light swat. She quivered with pleasure. "Deacon!" she gasped. "Please!"

Yes. Oh yes. She belonged to me. She belonged to Danny. But she belonged to Deacon even more. I reached around and stroked her breast as I plunged inside of her. She let out a quivering sigh as she stretched for me. God. She was so tight, she felt like a virgin. I knew instantly that she *had* waited. There'd been no one inside her but me. All this time. She was still mine. She was so slick, her tight little walls stretched for me and I found my way home.

I couldn't be gentle. Later, I would be. And there would be a later. Now that I'd had a taste, I wouldn't be able to let her go. I was strong once, I couldn't be again.

Beth bucked against me, drawing me deeper. Again, her movements were awkward, reckless. I pounded inside of her, filling her all the way. The pull between us made me see stars. I reached for her, stroking her swollen little clit as I thrust ever deeper.

"Deacon!" She screamed my name. Yes. This. Yes.

I flipped her. Beth went on her back and drew her knees up. A feral growl ripped from me as I caught sight of her like that. Her body responded to mine as if she were made for me. She reached for me, closing her fingers around my pulsing shaft.

"I want you," she whispered. "Oh God. I've never stopped wanting you."

I leaned down and caught her lips in a kiss. "I've thought about you every day. Dreamed about you every night, baby."

"Yes!" she whispered. "Oh. Yes. Don't stop. Danny, I don't care. Please just don't ever stop!"

Then she guided me back inside of her and wrapped her legs around my waist. So I took her there on the floor in the middle of her living room. Ten years ago, our first coupling had been fueled by grief and desperation as much as lust. There was some of that today, but it was so much more. Over and over, the truth washed over me. Beth was mine. She was *mine*! She was born for me and I was born for her.

I dug my fingers into the plush carpet. Beth arched her back and drew me in even closer. Her nails raked across my back, spurring me on. I fucked her deep, rattling her teeth. She matched me thrust for thrust.

Finally, my own need reached its zenith. Beth grabbed my ass and pulled me to her. I threw my head back and grunted as I poured my need inside of her. She took in every drop, whispering my name. I grabbed her ankles and drew them up over her head, spreading her so damn wide.

She was mine. Oh God. Mine! I would take her, claim her,

mark her as my own. If I went to hell for it, it would all be worth it. Every second.

Beth came again. I felt her walls twitch with pleasure and her eyes rolled back in her head. I held her legs wide apart as she floated down. God. I loved watching her like this. I felt like I could do it for the rest of my life.

Me and Beth. Beth and me. I've killed for her. I've lied for her. And I would sell my soul for her again if that's what it took.

Later, we stood under the shower together. I'd fucked and claimed her in the living room. I made love to her under the warm jets. I washed her hair and she washed mine. I watched the warm, soapy water sluice between her breasts and reached for her. Her pink nipples rose for me and I took each one in my mouth. Then a wicked glint came into her eye and she dropped to her knees. I dug my fingers into the grout as she took me in her mouth and made me come again.

After we dried off, we slept for a little while. Well, she slept; I watched her. She slept on her stomach with her perfect round ass slightly in the air. It drove me mad with lust again, but she needed her rest. In the cold light of day, she'd have a decision to make. I knew she might hate me a little for asking it.

When she woke, she made scrambled eggs. I sat in her little breakfast nook with a towel draped around my waist. Beth wore a short, satin robe and I had plans to get her out of it as soon as she stepped away from the stove. I had a million things to say to her, but so far we'd let our bodies do all the talking.

"What is it?" she finally said as she slid a pile of eggs onto a plate for me. When she moved to sit in the opposite chair, I reached for her and drew her into my lap. I pressed my nose between her breasts, inhaling her intoxicating, clean scent.

"Deacon, what is it?" she asked.

"Beth, I want you to get out of town for a little while. Just until we get a handle on the trouble that's coming."

She pursed her lips and set her fork down. When she slid off my lap and took her seat, I let her, even though my body still ached to hold her.

"Your trouble," she said. "It's got nothing to do with me."

I nodded. "It shouldn't. No. But if I'm right about Sean ..."

She held up a hand. "Sean was Sean. No matter what else ... he wasn't an innocent. You said the Hawks broke a rule by going after him. I don't think that's true. *Everyone* knew who Sean was mixed up with. Have there been any other family or friends of your club who have gotten hurt?"

"It's just a precaution," I said. "There's a safe house up the coast. I want to take you there. Get you out of sight while we handle this."

She looked me square in the eyes. "How are you going to handle this?"

I swallowed hard. "Beth, don't ask me that."

Her expression cooled. I realized my words had to sound an awful lot like what she'd heard from Sean. And I had to admit the danger that followed me now could be just as deadly.

"Fine," she said, rising. "I won't ask. Just like I refused to ask Sean. But this time, there's one glaring difference. Danny ... Deacon ... do what you have to do. But I'm through running."

With that, she gathered my plate and turned her back on me.

Chapter 11

BETH

As Deacon stood in my kitchen glaring at me, I did the one thing I hadn't done in more years than I could count. I called Darlene at the office and told her I'd be late.

"Take your time, honey," Darlene answered. "Haven't seen Ed yet and that's not a good sign."

My whole body just deflated. Dammit. He had a settlement conference this afternoon on an auto accident case. His fee from that was supposed to carry us through the next quarter. If he didn't show, the judge would have no choice but to enter a default against our client.

"What do you want me to do?" I asked. I felt like I was talking to two people at once. Deacon stood with clenched fists, his cold blue eyes filled with a protective fury. In his case, I knew his answer. He knew mine.

"Just live your life, Beth," Darlene said with a defeated sigh. "There's only so much either of us could do. I'm so tired of this. If my brother doesn't care enough to keep his head above water, I'm gettin' to the point where I'm done letting him drag me under."

I knew how she felt. Of course I did. The trouble was, ultimately Ed was the only one who could keep us in business.

"Okay," I answered. "I'll check back in a couple of hours. If anything changes let me know. I can try to call the judge's secretary and see if we can get another postponement."

"Don't bother," Darlene said. "I already tried that. The word's come down from the chief judge. No more postponements for any of Ed's cases."

"What? They can't do that."

"Yes, they can. I'm surprised they've waited this long. You know damn well that man has used up every second chance he had. Like I said, take some you time this morning. You've earned it. I'll figure out some way to keep the world from falling apart. I always do."

I knew Darlene could probably sense my sad smile as I said goodbye and hung up the phone. Deacon came to me the minute I put my phone on the counter.

My skin rippled with pleasure as he put his hands on my shoulders. He felt so good. His clean, musky scent filled my head, making me weak in the knees. I wanted him again. Plain and simple. I wanted to lose myself in his touch, give in to all the wicked dreams I'd had over the years. And there was the truth of it. I *had* dreamed of him all this time. I'd been kidding myself to think I was ever over Danny Wade.

"Come on," he said, trying a softer approach. This was more like the Danny I used to know. He could be hard and gentle all at the same time. He had a way of making a person feel safe and secure. Even before he started to pursue a life with the clergy, Danny was the guy everyone unloaded on. He listened without judgment. But that hard edge was there too, glistening in his pale blue eyes. Deacon Wade, patched member of the Dark Saints M.C. wasn't used to begging for anything.

"Danny," I said, sliding my hands up his arms. "I'm not going to run. Not anymore."

"I'm not asking you to run. Not like the last time. I'm just asking you to get out of town for a few days. I need to make sure you're safe."

I touched his face. His rough stubble tickled my fingertips. It got hard to think straight standing this close to him. "You said yourself, no one even knows I'm here but you."

"I said I *think* no one knows you're here but me. But people know *I'm* here. If they put two and two together, that could spell some trouble for you."

I dropped my hand. "I trust the people in this town, Danny. People like to gossip, but they also know when to mind their own business. Yes, you've been seen. And you've been seen with me. But this is Crystal Falls. There's no drug cartel here. The baddest element in town is ... well ... you."

Danny flinched, but didn't argue my point. He seemed on the verge of saying something else, but stopped.

"Tell me the truth," I said. I was about to ask a question I'd always avoided with Sean. "How bad is this thing with your club really going to get?"

He stepped away from me and walked toward the kitchen window. I had a small, square yard with a wooden privacy fence. There were some overgrown bushes in the north corner I'd been meaning to thin out.

"I don't know," he finally answered and I knew he spoke the truth. "I've never lived through a full club war. Most of our members haven't. The last major one happened before my time. Bear's kept us at peace for over twenty years. That's ... well ... it's unheard of in my line of work."

I slid my fingers up Danny's bare back. His jeans hung low on his hips. I was still getting used to the look of him. His rippling muscles were covered in tattoos. It shocked me at first; now in the light of day, it turned me on. The largest tattoo covered most of his back, a kneeling angel with great black wings unfurled behind it and a sword clasped in his hands. The Dark Saint. There were other symbols too, and dates. I traced the small rose on his bicep and the tiny date beneath it. His father's birthday. Instinct fueled me and I leaned over and kissed him there. A shiver went through Danny and he slid his arms around me.

"I think I'm glad you did it," I whispered. Tears sprang to my eyes, shocking me a little. Sean and Danny's father had been such a sweet, gentle man. He'd worked third shift at an oil refinery just outside of Port Azrael. Coleman Wade was nothing like my own father had been. He was steady, solid, pious. He made the Wade boys go to church every Sunday, no matter what. When Sean fell in with the cartel, Mr. Wade hadn't wanted to believe it. Neither did I. It was Danny who made us see the truth.

The night Mr. Wade died still burned in my heart. He'd been shot in my living room. A driveby. And it was my fault. They were looking for me and Sean. He would have been home, but I kicked him out the night before. Port Azrael was just as small as Crystal Falls when it came to everyone knowing your business.

"I shouldn't have made him leave," I whispered. Danny stiffened beside me. I hadn't meant to go there. I hadn't even given voice to it in all this time. It seemed this had been a day for confessions though and dealing with old wounds.

Danny turned to me. He hooked a finger beneath my chin and lifted my face until our eyes met again. "Then you would have been the one they killed," he said. I knew it. Of course I knew it. And yet, the guilt was still there.

"I wanted to kill him," I whispered. "I wanted Sean to pay for all the things he'd destroyed. Your father didn't deserve what happened to him. I wanted to make Sean hurt."

Danny's eyes narrowed. "Is that what I was?"

It wasn't fair and he knew it. It seemed he still had plenty of his own guilt to work through. I pulled away from him. "You know you weren't. But Sean never even knew that you and I ... that we ..."

"Beth," he said. "This is why I need you to get out of sight for a couple of days. I won't go through this again. I won't put you in the middle of another mess you didn't create."

I shook my head, trying to clear the shock at what he'd just said. "I'm already in the middle of it, Deacon. You put me in the middle of it the second you rode out here to find me. And before you take on the martyr role again, I'm not sorry you did."

I wanted to tell him how much I'd missed him. It was something I wasn't sure I was fully ready to admit to myself yet. I'd lived with a hole in my life. I'd filled it with other things. Work. Looking after Ed Albright. But I was starting to understand the shape of that hole more than I ever did. It was Danny. It was Deacon. And it scared the hell out of me.

Something changed in Danny. His posture straightened and his face took on that hard edge. That was the thing that was most different about him. It wasn't the tiny age lines around his eyes or even the tattoos. He had a roughness to his core that may have been there all along, only now it was exposed. I can't help that it thrilled me a little.

Danny brushed past me, walking with purpose. He went to the bedroom and pulled open my closet door.

"What are you doing?" I said, running to catch up with him.

"I told you, I won't go through it again. I won't put you at risk.

You are *going* to the safehouse, Beth. If I have to drag you kicking and screaming."

"No!" My shout cut through the air. Deacon froze. He'd found a leather backpack in the bottom of my closet and gripped it tight.

"No," I said softer. "I'm not running. I'm staying right here. I gave up everything. You can't ask me to do it again."

He pursed his lips so tight the blood left them. Tossing the backpack to my bed, he came to me. "It won't be forever. A few days. That's all."

"Don't. Don't promise me that. You've done that before, remember?"

God. It seemed I was on some merry-go-round. We'd had almost the exact same conversation the evening of Mr. Wade's funeral. Danny promised to keep me safe. I just had no idea how he'd planned to keep that particular oath.

"I'm safer here," I said. "You said yourself, it's my connection to you that puts me at risk. How can you be sure this safehouse you have really is safe? Deacon, I don't know your people. I know mine. Crystal Falls are my people for now. I'll lay low if that's what you want, but I'm not running. I've sacrificed too much for Sean ... and ... for you ... You can't make me do it again."

My words came out in a flood. I hadn't even planned what I'd say, but once they were out, I knew how deeply I meant them. As good as Danny made me feel, I would not run again. Not even for him.

He threw the backpack on the bed. Once again, I was struck by the steel in his eyes. Nobody said no to Deacon Wade and the Dark Saints M.C. Except I just did.

"You should go," I said, as a hollow pit formed in my core. At the same time, a tiny flame flickered inside me, drawing me to him. I wanted him. Craved him. Even now, my sex quivered with the need for his touch. But I'd let passion rule my heart far too many times.

"Beth." He moved, reaching for me. I stepped away.

"No," I said. "I'm sorry, Danny. Do you know how badly I just want to chuck everything and run away with you? Because I do. I want to trust you. I want to get carried away with you. But I can't. Not this time. Too much has happened. I've made too many choices based on fear. I won't do it again. I've fought too hard to make a life for myself. I won't give it up. Not even for you."

He ran a hard hand over his face. God. I still knew him so well. He was angry. He felt helpless. But he knew I was right.

"I can't stay here, Beth. I have to handle things with my club."

"I know." My throat felt tight.

As if on cue, his cell phone vibrated in his back pocket. Squeezing his eyes tight, he answered it. I backed away, not wanting to hear too much. But it didn't matter, I could read the expression on his face. He would leave me. I asked him to. Still, it hurt like hell.

I walked back out to the kitchen. My own cell was ringing.

Darlene's picture popped up and a pit formed in my stomach. It was Ed. It couldn't be good news.

"I need you, love," she said. "I think I've worked out a solution to Ed's docket today, but you're going to have to come in and make some promises."

Nodding, I drew in a breath. "Okay. I'll be there within an hour."

Deacon stood behind me. I hung up with Darlene and turned to him. "Beth, I wish you wouldn't. I wish you'd stay out of sight."

"And I wish you'd stay right here. It looks like we're both running for trouble." I smiled up at him. I'd told Danny I wanted to fight for the life I'd built. And yet it burned in me to ask him to give up his. He couldn't any more than I could.

"Fine," he said, giving me a soft smile that melted me. "You win. But will you promise me you'll be careful? Don't go off anywhere by yourself. Stay in town or stay home. No new client meetings. Home before dark."

I gave him a salute. "Promise. Can you promise me that you'll be careful too?"

He smiled and slid his fingers through my hair. Leaning down, he kissed me. Heat snaked through my heart. Oh, I wanted him. I'd never stopped. But we both had to get back to the lives we'd built. I just prayed his wouldn't ruin him.

Chapter 12

Deacon

Ten years ago, I thought I'd given up my soul. I had. But not for the reasons I'd been telling myself. Beth was my soul. She was my heart and my breath. As I rode out of Crystal Falls, I felt the pain of her loss like a knife in the gut. How could I have been so stupid to think I could touch her again ... taste her ... and not want more?

Axle's words were ominous. I'd tried to play it off in Beth's living room, but she knew. She could see straight through me just like she always could. Bear was calling for a full meeting first thing in the morning. A few of the guys had already gotten their wives and women out of town. It was bad. I just prayed leaving Beth in Crystal Falls was the right thing.

I meant to get a quick shower and change of clothes as I pulled into my driveway off Cliffside Drive. I had a little place overlooking the dunes. Not an ocean view, but you could hear it this far out. My heart dropped when I saw the tan sedan parked at the curb. I pulled my Harley into the garage and drew my Nine.

The house was empty, but the sliding door to the wooden deck I'd built in the back stood open. Squaring my shoulders, I took a breath to steel myself against what I knew was coming.

"You trying to let all the flies in?" I asked, stepping out onto the deck. Father Sanchez sat cross-legged, staring out at the sandscape. He'd brought a bottle of wine and helped himself to one of my glasses. I'd asked Toby, one of the probies, to keep an eye on my place while I was gone. It probably took all of two seconds for Father Sanchez to get him to tell him where I kept the spare key.

"I'm trying to let the air in," he said, sipping his wine. "It gets stuffy in there all closed up."

I tossed my keys on the wrought iron patio table and took a seat beside him. Father Sanchez tilted the wine bottle toward me. He had an empty glass waiting. I waved it off.

"Ah," he said. "Still only a sip of church wine on Sundays for you?"

I swallowed hard. "Something like that." Of course, Diego Sanchez knew just how long it had been since I graced one of his pews at San Mateo's.

"Well, you found me," I said. Father never liked to be rushed.

He stayed in control by staying silent. It was an old trick he used with parishioners. Let them do ninety-nine percent of the talking and they walk away thinking you're wise as Yoda.

"I've been worried about you, son," he said.

"I'd have thought you had a congregation full of souls to save, Father. You know mine's a lost cause."

He laughed softly and set down his glass. "That's what you like to tell yourself. Though, I know you don't believe it."

I squirmed in my chair. I didn't want to be rude, but the old man's timing was lousy. He'd argue it was entirely perfect.

"Look," I said. "I appreciate you taking the time to check in on me. And I could tell you I'm fine and you won't believe it. And we can do the dance we always do. But I can't do it now. I need to get to the clubhouse."

He nodded. "You've been away a lot. That's not like you. Especially now."

"What do you mean by that?"

Sanchez turned. He leveled his dark eyes at me. When I was a kid, that look used to turn my spine to water. It was as if he could see straight through to my soul. I could never lie to him back then. I didn't try now. But there were some things that just weren't this old man's business anymore.

He folded his hands in his lap. "Fine. Deacon."

He never called me that. It was either Daniel, or son. He'd

accepted my choice to leave the priesthood, more or less. But I knew he took the patch I now wore as a personal betrayal. Even if he couldn't bring himself to say it.

"I see things," he said. "And I'm an old man. Too old to go through this shit again."

I blanched. My whole life, I'd never heard Father Sanchez swear. Anger swirled behind his eyes. "I don't know what you mean."

He slammed his fist against the table, nearly overturning it. "Don't. Save both our dignity and don't lie to me. I'm not asking for details. It's probably better if I don't hear them, even within the confines of the confessional."

"I don't recall asking for absolution," I said.

"No," he said. "You haven't. Not this time. And I didn't say I'd be inclined to give it."

This got an eye raise out of me. "Don't tell me you're the one having trouble keeping your vows this time." I meant it almost as a joke. Banter was one of the things we did best. But Sanchez wasn't smiling.

"I told you. I'm old, Daniel. Too old. And I know what's going on. You and your crew are about to let this town go to hell. For what? Guns? Drugs? Money?"

"The Saints don't deal drugs and you know it," I said, anger rising.

Sanchez waved a dismissive hand. "Spare me the finer points. Was Sean the opening shot? Was it the Devils Hawks?"

I cleared my throat. "That would fall under the heading of a finer point, Father."

"You're young," he said. "All of you. You have no idea the kind of destruction a club war would do to this town. People will die, Deacon. Innocent people. People you love. People *I* love. Even if you win."

"You know I can't discuss this with you."

"No," he said. "Of course not. And I don't recall asking you to."

"Then what are you here for? Are you going to try and convince me to leave the club?"

Father Sanchez reached for his wine. "I know what happens because I've seen it, Daniel. You're willing to let this town burn, for what? More territory? You never pay the price. We're the ones that pay the price."

I leaned forward; the worn leather of my cut creaked. "It's not just about territory. If you've seen what you say you have, you know that too. Like it or not, my club is what keeps even worse evil from getting in."

"There is no worse evil, Daniel. There's just evil."

I laughed. "And if you really believed that, you wouldn't be sitting here."

"Did it help?" he asked, not missing a beat.

"Did what help?"

He took a slow sip. "Revenge. When you turned to it. Did it

fill the hole in your heart? Did it bring your father back to you?"

I squeezed my eyes shut and clenched a fist. "I told you, I didn't ask you to hear my confession."

"No. You didn't. You haven't asked me that in years. And I couldn't absolve you anyway, probably. Because I believe you'd do it again. You're getting ready to."

"Don't," I said, placing a hand over Father Sanchez's when he reached for his wine. "Why don't you just come out with it? What are you really doing here?"

He snatched his hand away. "I don't know. That's the God's honest truth. No. Maybe it isn't. I'm worried. I'm an old man, and I know war is coming to Port Azrael again. And I know you're going to be at the center of it. So I was hoping, futile though that may be, that I could convince you not to be."

"You're right. Probably about all of it. But mostly about the futility. I'm where I'm supposed to be. I know that disappoints you."

He poured himself another glass of wine. If he had any more, I'd need to call him a cab. "Where's that, Daniel? I think maybe that's what I'm doing here. You disappeared after Sean died. Where?"

I turned from him. A breeze picked up, sending spirals of sand across the landscape. He knew me. Damn the man, he still knew me so well.

"Is she well?" he asked. I didn't want to answer. Father Sanchez had counseled Beth as much as me when we learned the truth about Sean. And he'd been the first to see what grew between us. He also knew I wouldn't be strong enough to walk away.

"Well enough," I finally said, growing angry. If he started to lecture me about the past, I might just throw him out. He didn't though.

"I miss her too," he said, sighing. "Beth was ... well, she was special, wasn't she?"

I didn't have to answer him. He could see the truth in my eyes. Yes, she was special. She was everything.

"But even she wasn't enough to keep you from breaking your vows."

I tapped my fingers on the table. Vows. I'd taken so many in my life. I'd kept the ones that mattered most. To my club. To the brothers I chose, if not the one I was born with. And I would keep my vow to Beth.

"I used to think she was the reason you turned away from your calling," he said. "Temptation of the flesh. I couldn't blame you. Either of you, really. Sean betrayed you both. It was only natural that you should turn to each other. It was *my* idea that she seek counsel from you. I thought you could help each other."

Something hardened inside of me. What Beth and I shared had been more sacred than anything that ever happened in church for me. "We did," I said. There was no point denying what we were to each other back then. I had confessed that sin to this man long ago.

"So," Father Sanchez said, finishing the last of his wine. "She took you back, did she?"

"Back?"

He eyed me up and down. The man had a way of reading my soul that set the hairs on the back of my neck on end. Once upon a time, I felt I couldn't hide anything from him. Now I knew I could. He knew it too.

"I figured you'd go to her once Sean was out of the way."

"It was never about Sean," I snapped.

He nodded. "Have it your way. Does Beth know what's coming? With the club?"

I didn't answer.

"Son," he said, reaching for me again. "You think I don't understand what's churning inside of you? You think I've lived a chaste life? I'm a man. I've had my own temptations. My own demons."

"And I told you, I'm not looking for absolution."

He squeezed my arm. "And I told you I'm not here to give it. But know this: it's not too late for you. Even with everything you've done. Everything you're about to do. Beth though ... You cannot drag her through this. If you do, every sacrifice you've made, every oath you've broken, it will be for nothing."

"What are you asking me?" I pulled my hand away. "You speak in riddles, old man. I don't have time for it. I have to get to the clubhouse."

He sighed. "Of course you do. There'll be a vote to take, I expect. A pretty big one, eh?"

I wouldn't answer. What was there to say?

"Do you love her?" he asked, throwing me.

Love. It almost seemed an inadequate word for what my heart felt toward Beth. It was so big I couldn't describe it. I certainly couldn't explain it to someone like Father Sanchez who'd lived his life alone.

"Well," he said. "Whatever she is to you, open your eyes, if not your heart, to what's to come. No matter what you tell yourself. No matter what you tell her, she can't be safe through this."

"I think you should go."

He shrugged. "I probably should. But I told you, I miss Beth too. And I care about her. We love some of the same people. So I'm asking you. No, I'm telling you. If you *do* love her, don't drag her through this. She survived Sean. She won't survive you."

"What do you want me to do?" I snapped, though his answer was obvious. It burned in my heart like a brand.

Father Sanchez smiled as he slowly rose. He put a hand on my shoulder in almost a benediction. "If you love her, son. You have to let her go."

With that, he turned and left.

Chapter 13

Beth

My heels clicked against the marble floors as I hit a dead run into the emergency room. It was the only part of Darlene's message that made any sense. It also wasn't the first time and likely not the last she'd call me out here in the middle of the night.

I found her slumped over in a waiting room chair, face in hands. Her cheeks were bright red. No, almost purple, as she took great, heaving breaths. One of the nurses stood beside her, rubbing her back. Janet, I think her name was. We'd represented her son a few years ago when he got caught drinking underage at a neighborhood party. He'd turned out all right. Kept out of trouble after that and got a lacrosse scholarship to a small college in the panhandle.

Janet met my eyes and gave me a tight-lipped smile. She

whispered something into Darlene's ear then gently excused herself. Darlene didn't look up as I took the seat beside her and took up where Janet left off, rubbing Darlene's back.

"Is he okay?" I asked, almost afraid to hear the answer.

"He started coughing up blood," Darlene said. My heart dropped. "Sadie called. Found him slumped over his steering wheel an hour ago."

"His steering wheel? How the hell did Ed even have a set of keys? Sadie usually makes him surrender them before she'll serve him even one drink."

Darlene blew her nose into a tissue, sounding like a strangled goose. "Oh, he didn't have keys. He was sleeping in his car, is all."

"What do the doctors say?"

Darlene finally looked up at me, her eyes puffy from crying. My heart went out to her. Ed was her whole life. She'd been married a half a dozen times but Ed had always been her number one project. Her lost cause.

"It's his liver," she said. "It was always going to be his liver. Plus his blood pressure is through the roof and just about every other thing."

"He'll pull through," I said. "He always does. We'll get him into that rehab place. He'll dry out. We've been through this before, Dar. It's going to be okay."

"He's not getting any younger," she said. "And neither am I. I'm done, Beth. I just can't keep doing this. Neither can you. I told him as much. Judge Dupree told him he doesn't want to see him in his courtroom again until he gets his act together. If he ever can. He means it this time. They're going to report him to the state bar."

I sat back in my chair. Of course, I'd been through this routine with both Darlene and Ed enough over the last ten years. Something seemed altogether different though. Darlene just looked ... old. Worn out. Cleaning up after Ed was no kind of life for her long term and we both knew it.

"You deserve something else," she said, as if reading my mind.

"Don't worry about me," I said. "You know I can take care of myself."

"Hmmm. I don't know about that." Darlene honked one more time into her tissue. It helped. Her eyes cleared and she put something resembling a smile on her face. Stuffing the tissue in her pocket, she put a hand over mine.

"Did you enjoy your half a day off?" There was a mischievous twinkle in her eye. I wondered how long Darlene had been waiting to steer the subject to my personal life. Even in her distress, the woman never missed a beat.

Doctor Perkins saved me from having to answer her right away. The guy looked about a hundred years old and had been an E.R. attending at Crystal Falls Hospital for as long as anyone could remember. He knew everyone's business, of course, but never gossiped.

"He's coming around," Doctor Perkins said. He put a soft

hand on Darlene's shoulder and smiled down at her. He shot me a quick wink. Darlene made another choked-goose sound then hiccupped.

"We'll get him through this crisis, Darlene," Perkins said. "But longer term, we can't keep going this way. I've talked to Ed and he's saying the right things. I'll take that as progress. Usually, all he does is crack jokes. I think this episode scared him. That could be a good thing."

"Can I see him?" Darlene asked.

"In a little while. He's sleeping right now and that's the best thing for him. I've got him on IV fluids. We'll get those electrolytes under control. He'll feel a lot better in a few hours. But how about you? You don't look so good yourself."

Darlene waved him off. "You flatterer, you."

"I'll make sure she gets home," I said. "As long as you think Ed's stable enough so that we won't run into any surprises tonight."

Perkins shook his head. "Nah. He's snoring to wake the dead. We'll get him moved to a regular room. Things will look brighter tomorrow. We can go over some aftercare options. There's a clinic in Corpus Christi that I want him to think seriously about. Get him dried out and thinking clearer. When I mentioned it, he seemed interested."

"It's a plan," I said. "Thank you."

Doctor Perkins winked at me again and squeezed Darlene's

shoulder. "I meant what I said, Darlene. Get home. Get some rest. We'll pull Ed through this just like always."

"He's not getting any younger and neither am I." She sighed.

"Yeah. Me neither. But let's not try to solve the world's problems all at once, okay? One thing at a time. Sleep for you. Sleep for Ed. Then we'll talk."

I stood up and shook Doctor Perkins's hand. Another nurse called him away and he gave Darlene a quick hug before leaving us alone. I gathered her purse and stood tapping my foot.

"Come on," I said. "I'll walk you to your car. I'm not letting you sleep in this waiting room tonight. You heard Doctor Perkins. There's no need. Ed's in good hands. We'll come up with a game plan tomorrow."

With great effort, Darlene got to her feet. She looped her arm through mine and we headed for the parking lot.

"And you didn't answer my question," she said. "What about *your* game plan?"

"What do you mean?" There was no way I'd make it out of here scot-free now. The truth was, I was worried. Yes. We'd been down this road with Ed plenty. But something was different in Darlene's eyes. I believed her when she said she'd reached the end of her rope.

"Come on," she said. We'd reached her car. Darlene drove a red Dodge Charger. It was her pride and joy. She parked it in as secluded a spot in the lot as she could. The woman could move fast, as long as she didn't have to take stairs. "Give me a spot of bright news today, Beth."

I readjusted the weight of my purse on my shoulder. It had been a long day. I'd spent most of it in the office alone, catching Ed up on all his research and deposition prep. Now all that was up in the air again. My heart sank knowing I'd spend tomorrow trying to rearrange his docket. Again. Our hardcore, loyal clients could be patient. But we'd lose business over Ed's latest hospital stint. No question.

"What do you want me to say?" I smiled.

Darlene put a hand on my shoulder. "That guy. Deacon. I checked him out."

"What do you mean, you checked him out?"

She leaned against her car door. "Oh, come on. It wasn't hard. He's the club chaplain for the Saints. I have eyes and I can read. I asked around. He's a mystery man, honey. Kinda like you. Most of those boys over in Port Azrael have a reputation. Or at least they did before they started settling down. But that one, Deacon? He's single. Doesn't cut loose like the rest of them. Honey, he's gorgeous. So, what are you doing?"

My throat went dry. I didn't want to lie to Darlene, but I was far from ready to discuss my relationship with Deacon. Relationship. I didn't even know if that's what I could call it. We left things in limbo. He'd stopped asking me to get out of town, but things were far from settled between us. I didn't even know for sure if I'd see him again. My heart skipped a beat as I let the thought settle in. What if I never saw him again?

"Oh man," Darlene said. "I don't think I've ever seen you like this."

"Like what?"

She put two firm hands on my shoulders and gave me a gentle shake. "Starstruck, honey. That man's got you stirred up and twisted. Oh, I know the feeling. Reminds me of my first husband, Mattie. He was in a club too. Did I ever tell you that?"

I blinked hard, trying to picture a young Darlene on the back of a Harley. From the misting in her eyes, I knew she was picturing the same thing. "He was a road captain for the Great Wolves M.C. out of Emerald Pointe. God. That was a million years ago. We weren't married long. Not even a year. Oh, but it was a hell of a year."

"Pictures or it didn't happen," I said, trying to keep the subject pointed at her instead of me. She wasn't letting go, though.

"Honey, I'm the last person to give anyone else advice on men. But that one's got a hold of you right here." She pointed her finger straight at my heart.

"Darlene, I just can't ..."

She put up a hand. "Don't bother. I know you don't like

talking about your personal life. It's just nice to see you have one. I said I shouldn't give advice but I'm going to anyway. Live a little. Take some time off. Climb on the back of that hog and let him take you for a ride. Even if he breaks your heart."

I leaned in and gave her a hug. "Thanks. But I don't know what's going on with him or with me."

"As long as I'm the first to know when you figure it out."

I gave her a quick salute as Darlene opened her car door and climbed inside. "And don't come here tomorrow," she said. "Take the day off. Go to Port Az or up the coast or somewhere that's not here. I'll deal with my brother. And all the drama will still be here when you get back. That's a promise."

Darlene's light laughter warmed my heart. She slammed her car door shut and turned the ignition. I stepped back as she roared out of her parking space and took the curve toward the exit way too fast.

I hugged myself and headed up the ramp toward my own car. Deacon's blue eyes swam before me as I made my way through town. Should I call him? We'd left things so unsettled. I wanted to see him again. That much was clear. Maybe Darlene was right. Maybe it was worth taking a chance even if Deacon broke my heart.

It was still pitch dark out when I pulled into my driveway. I cut the ignition and sat there for a moment. The house was dark and quiet but I didn't know if I'd be able to sleep. I checked my phone, but Deacon hadn't called. I had a glass of wine waiting in the fridge and right then it sounded like heaven.

As I went through the garage, something didn't seem right. The storm door was shut but the heavy wooden door leading to the basement was wide open. I set my purse on the kitchen counter and started flicking lights on.

I made it as far as the living room before a hand clamped over my mouth and dragged me back into the kitchen. I felt suspended in time as I tried to kick backward. The intruder was huge and strong; the scent of sweat and leather filled my nostrils. I bit down on the fleshy part of his hand. It was like biting steel.

He shoved me into the living room. I stumbled forward like a rag doll, bracing myself against the far wall. He was on me again, pressing his knee between my legs so I couldn't kick back. He smashed my face against the wall. His breath came hot in my ear.

"Took me ten seconds to break that lock on your back door," he said, his voice deep and gravelly. I squeezed my eyes shut past the tears that instantly sprang to them.

"I have money in my purse," I said. "Take it. Then get out."

He laughed. "Ain't after money, sweetie. Just want to make sure you hear me loud and clear."

I strained against him, but it was like trying to move two hundred pounds of granite. "I'm listening," I gasped. Adrenaline coursed through me, making me light-headed. I could *not* faint. A million lessons from self-defense classes ran through my head. Don't leave with him, no matter what.

I drew in a breath, getting ready to scream. He shoved me harder against the wall.

"Not gonna hurt you ... yet," he said. "You tell your boyfriend I came here, I'll slit your throat while you sleep. I got to you once. I can do it again. No matter where you are. Got it?"

"Yes!" I hissed. "What the hell do you want?"

"Just a warning," he said. "You need to be careful the company you keep. Woman like you could get hurt. I'd hate to see that happen. Mrs. Wade."

He paused before saying my name. My heart raced. Was he here about Sean or Deacon? Before I could ask, he licked my cheek with his rough tongue. My stomach turned.

"We're watching you. Don't ever forget that. We can get to you. We've always been able to get to you. At work. At home. Anywhere you think you can run. Remember that."

"What? I don't know what you even want from me."

He laughed against my ear. "Just want you to know that. You're only safe because we let you be. Won't always."

"I get it," I said. Though fear raced through me, some logical part of my brain told me if he were here to really hurt me, he would have done it already.

"Have a nice day," he said, shoving me hard to the floor. I shielded my eyes, expecting him to grab me again. But my attacker went straight out the front door, slamming it behind him. I scrambled to my feet. The motion light went on. The guy didn't turn back but I could read the symbol and patch on the back of his leather vest plain as day.

Devils Hawks M.C.

He shook out his dirty blond hair then disappeared into the shadows on the other side of the street.

Chapter 14

Deacon

THE DAY after Father Sanchez's visit, Bear called a meeting. A hard knot formed in my stomach as I rode up to the clubhouse. I was the last to get there. He'd called it for midnight. A full moon hung low in the sky. Even Rufus seemed to know something was about to change. He usually charged around the side of the building when one of us rode up. Tonight, he sat vigil in front of the door, his crooked ears pricked. Not even Mama Bear came out to greet me. It meant Bear had sent her away.

I cut my engine and parked. Beth was still heavily on my mind. The priest's words had settled over me, but I could barely process them. Let Beth go. Of course that was the safest thing to do. I'd done it before. She was better off without me. And yet, the thought of leaving her behind tore at me, making it hard to breathe.

I dismounted and headed for the front door. Before I got there, the shadows moved. Axle and Shep came around the other side of the building. Axle stepped under the floodlight, looking like a damn ghost. As club enforcer, the man was paid to look dangerous. In his case, he did more than just look the part. He fixed a hard stare at me and a look passed between him and Shep.

"You're late," Axle said, his voice gruff.

"I'm here," I answered. I'd take that kind of shit from Bear, but not Axle. Not tonight. I tried to walk past them, but Axle reached out and put a hand on the center of my chest, stopping me.

"We need to talk," he said.

"And I think Bear's waiting," I answered. I didn't like the look in Axle's eyes.

"Where've you been, man?" he asked. Axle's cheekbone was still swollen from his run-in the other day. Shep looked none the worse for wear, but he kept his arm in a sling beneath his leather cut.

"I've had some personal business I needed to take care of," I said. These men were my brothers, but I still had secrets I needed to keep. They didn't know about Beth. They didn't know what I'd done to prove my loyalty to Bear all those years ago. For now, I still felt the fewer people knew about Beth, the better chance I could keep her clear of the danger that might come.

"You've been gone a lot lately," Shep said. "Your timing's lousy, Deacon."

I reared back. Where the hell was this coming from? As far as I was concerned, only Bear needed to know where I was. And he did. So why were Shep and Axle busting my balls about it?

"I told you, I've had some personal business that couldn't wait."

"We're your business," Axle said, his eyes flashing. "Now's not the time for any of us to be going off on any side projects."

"What the hell, man," I said. "What I do on my downtime isn't for you to worry about. Bear knows what's up. That's all that matters. Now if it's all the same to you, I wanna get inside. Last time I checked, Bear was president of this club, not you."

Axle's face changed. I knew what threw him. I was the peacemaker. Everyone's confessor. He hadn't expected a pushback like this from me. Tough shit. I had my own problems to deal with. For once, Axle and the others would have to look elsewhere for someone to lean on.

"It's just not a good idea for anybody to go disappearing on their own, Deacon," Shep said. All of a sudden, he picked up the peacemaker role. "Look what happened to Axle and me and we had each other's six."

"Well, I'm sorry about that," I said. "But for now, I know how to take care of myself. Now, do you have more shit to give me or are we ready to go inside?"

"You ladies done gossiping?" E.Z.'s raspy voice cut through the air. He swung the front door open and glared at Shep. "We're at the table!"

I didn't wait for Shep or Axle to answer him. I brushed past E.Z. and headed into the clubhouse wondering what the hell that was all about. Axle held some kind of accusation in his eyes. Under other circumstances, that might have mattered. But the vibe in the room drove out any worry I had about it.

The rest of the crew were assembled at the conference table. Bear had cleared the rest of the clubhouse. Mama was gone, so were the prospects. Whatever happened here tonight, this was members only. I took my seat at the end of the table and waited for Axle and Shep to file in. When they did, Bo and Maddox shifted in their seats. The four of them exchanged a look then settled their stares at me. What the actual hell? There was a meeting about to take place, but I couldn't shake the feeling that something else was swirling around with those four.

Bear wasted no time on preamble. "We've got trouble, boys," he said. "I was hoping the little dust-up Shep and Axle ran into last week would be just that. But as of now, we've lost the confidence of our main gun supplier up the coast. I had a sit-down this morning and it didn't go well."

There were grumblings through the room but this was no surprise. I folded my hands in front of me and rested my elbows on the table.

"So we go over their head," Zig said. "Let me rattle some cages and get the DiSalvo family involved." Zig had married into one of the biggest crime families in the country. But even that kind of weight might not be enough to sway things if any more momentum shifted away from us.

No sooner had I thought it before Bear broke even worse news. "We're losing contracts along the docks," he said. "Businesses are pulling out. They don't want anything to do with us when the shit hits the fan. We're in a worst-case scenario."

"You happy now?" E.Z. said it under his breath but the entire table heard it. This had been coming on for a very long time. E.Z. had been spoiling for war for months. It was Bear's steady hand at the helm that had kept us from it. Now I knew more men at this table shared E.Z.'s sentiment.

"What do we know?" Chase asked.

"Our suppliers had a sit-down with A.J. Moss," Bear said. His face turned ashen. Moss had been voted in as the Hawks' president a few months ago.

"Well, that sure as shit didn't take long," E.Z. said, banging his fist against the table. "How many times did I have to say it? I know you wanted to give the guy the benefit of the doubt, but the minute their old prez got forced out, we were set on this path, Bear. You know it and I know it."

Bear leaned back in his chair. He scratched his chin and let E.Z. rant. Sometimes, it was the best way to deal with him. E.Z. got to his feet and started to pace. "Half the guys under him hate his guts," E.Z. said. "The only thing they hate more are the men in this room. A.J. needed this war to unite his club and you know it. But no, you tried to work with him!"

Bear was cool. He just stared at E.Z. with his killer eyes. "You're damn right. And I'd make the same moves again if I had to do it over. The risk was worth taking. It just didn't fall how we wanted. And here we are."

"You gonna tell them the rest of it, or should I?" E.Z.'s voice rose even higher. In another minute, Bear might literally smack him down if he didn't get a hold of himself. Shep looked ready to pop a vein in his neck. If E.Z. made even the slightest move toward Bear, he'd get his throat ripped out.

Bear looked straight at me. "Our contact at the Port Az P.D. called me an hour ago," he said. "About Sean's case. They found the shooter."

I reared back like he'd delivered a blow to my solar plexus. "Why the hell wasn't I on that call?"

"Because you weren't here," Shep answered. "Because lately you're *never* here!"

"Enough!" Bear shouted. "We will have unity at this table tonight." Bear met my eyes. "They've arrested Milo Higgins. A waitress at Digby's fingered him dumping something in the alley the night they found Sean. She stuck her neck out for us on this one. The cops have her in protective custody."

"Milo Higgins?" I said, not believing what I was hearing. Higgins was a patched-in member of the Laredo Hawks. Why in the hell would they let him get his hands dirty like this?

"They found the murder weapon and Milo's prints all over it," Bear said. "It's messy as hell and I don't understand it, but there's no mistake. Sean was a Hawks hit. It means they're changing the rules."

E.Z. finally took his seat. I couldn't breathe. The Hawks were changing the rules. They were going after families. Sure, Sean wasn't a civilian, but he was still my brother.

"So the path before us is pretty clear," Bear said. "But you all need to understand what this is going to mean for us if we go forward."

"If?" This time Axle said it. We were all thinking it.

"It's different now," Bear said. "Most of you have families, or old ladies. People you care about. The Hawks know it. They've proven they'll cross that line. Sean Wade was no choir boy, but he's Deacon's brother. That shit can't stand."

"Vote!" Zig shouted it. It drew a round of knocks across the table. Bear clenched the gavel in his fist. His face was hard as granite as he sat up straight and said the words.

"All right. We vote. We all know what we're here for. We're at war." He didn't even need to poll the table. A chorus of "Ayes" rose up. His knuckles white, Bear knocked the gavel against the table.

"We take it to them," E.Z. said, his eyes glinting with bloodlust. I can't help that it stirred mine too. Sean was my brother. Chances were, he'd have ended up just how he did no matter what. But he was *my* brother. And I'd already lost too much.

"You need to prepare yourselves," Bear said. "Those of you with wives and children, Port Az won't be safe for them for now. Nobody at this table travels alone again unless you clear it with me first. If you don't have someplace safe to send your women to, send them here. The clubhouse is on lockdown until further notice. Only essential travel. We're gonna hit 'em back hard. You need to be ready for it. No mistakes."

Bear's eyes met mine. "Time to tie up loose ends," he said. "And everyone get their affairs in order. I don't want to lose a single person at this table, but you know I can't promise that. This is going to rip Port Azrael apart."

Father Sanchez's exact same words burned through me. He was cautious. He was scared. I wasn't. My fingers itched to pull the trigger of my Nine. The same thirst for revenge burned through me as the day I found my father's bullet-riddled body. No matter what, I would protect what was mine. Even if it meant I had to send Beth away again. She'd have no choice. I would not lose her. Not like Sean. Not like my father. If I didn't walk away from this, she would. So help me God.

War had come to Port Azrael. I knew none of our lives or this club would ever be the same again.

Chapter 15

BETH

"That ought to do you, ma'am."

I stood with my arms folded against the far wall. The van in my driveway drew a crowd. Paul Sauter owned the only locksmith/home security business in town. He punched buttons on the keypad he'd just installed near the front door then snapped the box closed.

"Hit your code then enter if you want to shut it off. When it goes off, it'll send a signal to our computers and then trip the 911 system. So if you don't mean for it to go off, get in here and enter your credentials within sixty seconds."

"Thanks, Paul," I said. I signed the work order and let him out. The alarm system beeped once when I shut the door. I opened it again to make sure the thing was armed. As Paul backed his van out of the driveway, the gawkers across the street started to disperse. There was nothing to do now but go to work, such as it was.

Ed had been discharged from the hospital and Darlene was driving him to a rehab facility up the coast. My job was to head back to the courthouse and file motions on all his outstanding hearings. Then I had to try and smooth things over with the clients we had on the front burner. This time, there'd be no help for it. I would have to make arrangements for substitute counsel. Ed's drinking had finally caught up with him. We were losing business.

I had three missed calls from Deacon and no idea what to do. The asshole who broke into my house made sure I saw his patch and knew exactly where he was from. If he didn't really want Deacon to know about it, why on earth would he have made a point of all that? Only one thing made any sense. He *wanted* me to run to Deacon right away. He was trying to play us both. If I told Deacon a Hawk broke into my house and threatened me, Deacon and the club would retaliate.

After smoothing over what I could at the courthouse, I started back for the office. I made it as far as the town square before Sheriff Finch flagged me down.

"Hey, Beckett," I said, painting on a smile. He had that concerned look in his eye as he crossed the street and came to me.

"Hey, yourself. Haven't seen you around much. Everything going okay with Ed?"

I adjusted the strap on my messenger bag. Beckett took me by the arm and led me to one of the park benches near the water fountain at the center of town. So this wasn't going to just be a casual hello. I chewed my bottom lip and sat down.

"Ed is Ed," I answered. "He's getting some help. Hopefully it sticks this time."

"Well, I sure hope so. Despite all his shortcomings, Ed Albright is one of the good ones."

I don't know why, but Beckett's words brought a lump to my throat. I'd spent so much time covering for and defending Ed, it was nice to have someone else see past all his ... shortcomings ... for a change.

"I've been meaning to check in on you," he said. "And look, I told you last time that I don't relish stepping into your business, but I'm hoping you know you can come to me if you ever need anything."

"Beckett, I appreciate it. I really do. And I hope *you* don't take this the wrong way, but I don't really need you to step into my business. If that changes, I know how to ask for help. Promise."

I knew he wasn't satisfied with my answer. I also knew he'd probably already heard I had Paul's security company at the house this morning. Life in a small town, I guess. Beckett Finch was also one of the good ones. There was no doubt in my mind enough people had seen me with Deacon for it to get back to Beckett. It wasn't jealousy swirling in his eyes though, it was deep concern.

"Well," he said, tipping his hat to me. "Then I won't keep you.

Except for one thing. I've heard some rumblings that have me worried. It's the only reason I'm even willing to step over the line with you."

"What rumblings?" I asked, shielding my eyes from the sun. Beckett had stood up and I looked up at him.

Squinting, he stared at a far-off point before answering. "Look, I don't know if that guy from the Saints is a close friend of yours or a casual acquaintance. And I know neither is any of my damn business, Beth. But I have it on good authority that things are about to hit the fan with that club and the one over in Laredo. People are going to get hurt. I just want to do everything in my power to make sure it's none of *my* people."

I rose and slid my bag over my shoulder. "And you consider me one of your people?"

He gave me a crooked smile. "Well, Beth, yes, I do. So does the rest of Crystal Falls. The trouble with men like Deacon Wade, there's always collateral damage."

Beckett dropped his smile and his words cut straight through me. He *had* done his research. I never once told him Deacon's name. I didn't have to. Damn this small town.

"Noted," I said, my heart racing. "I'll watch my back." It was in me to tell Beckett about what happened last night. The thing was, he already knew something was up. Once again, I felt the need to protect Deacon. I just didn't know how best to do it. For now, I went with my gut. The fewer people involved in Deacon's business, the better.

I knew Beckett wasn't satisfied, but I couldn't help that for now. He let it drop and I walked to my car. My heart jumped as my phone rang in my bag. I pulled it out. Deacon. I felt that same little ache I always got when thinking about him.

"Hey," I answered. There was silence on the other end for a moment.

"Hey, you," he finally said.

I wanted to tell him it was good to hear his voice. It was. I wanted to fall apart and unload on him with everything that had happened. Still, something held me back. Maybe it was the stupidest thing I could have done under the circumstances, but I decided to trust my gut.

"I just wanted to make sure you were doing okay," he said. "I didn't like how we left things."

I squeezed the phone to my ear. "I wish you were here," I said, breathless. I meant to keep it cool, but everything that was in my heart just rushed out.

"I wish I was there too. Beth, that's what I need to talk to you about."

A lump formed in my throat. Oh, I knew this side of him all too well. It was the thing that drove me the most crazy about Danny when we were younger. He would open his heart, then turn to ice. Before, it was guilt and obligation. This time, he thought he was protecting me.

"I'm listening," I said.

"Baby. I ... I can't see you for a while. Things are ..."

His voice trailed off. Deacon's words echoed those of Beckett's. Something was already happening. "Don't say it," I finished for him. "I don't think I want to know."

"Look. I just need to know everything is okay with you. I can handle all the rest of it if I know that."

"Don't put this on me," I said, hating the hard edge my voice took. "I'm fine, Danny. I've been fine for ten years, remember?" God. We both knew that wasn't true.

"I wanted to come there and tell you all of this in person," he said. "It's just not a good idea today. There are some things going down and it might get messy. You know I can't go into detail. Especially not over the phone, but ..."

"Danny," I said, my voice cracking. My world spun. This had all happened before. He was saying the exact things Sean used to tell me. Things were messed up. He had it under control. He'd need me to just sit tight and wait for him. But this wasn't Sean, this was Danny. And here I was again.

"It's okay," I said, finding a cool tone. "I know how to take care of myself."

"I still wish you'd take a vacation. Just go be somewhere where nobody knows you for a little while."

"Can you promise me something?" I asked. "Can you promise me you'll be careful?"

The sigh on the other end of the phone cut through me. Oh God. This was *just* like it had been with Sean before everything turned to shit. Why couldn't I keep from falling for men who were no good for me?

"Yeah," he said. It was as good as I was going to get. "Beth ... you might not hear from me for a little while. And you might hear *about* some things you won't like."

"You voted to go to war," I whispered. Danny got silent again. "Danny? I'll go. Okay? If you come with me, I'll go. Whatever's about to happen, you don't have to be there. You took care of me. You took care of your family. If this is about Sean, he's not worth it. Not anymore. If he were here ... I swear I think he'd tell you to forget about what happened to him. He knew, you know? He always knew he'd end up just how he did."

"Beth, I've got to go."

"No, you don't!" I screamed into the phone and hated myself for that too. Old patterns. History repeating itself. If I closed my eyes, I could picture Danny lying dead in some alley instead of Sean. They were nothing alike. Sean had real evil in him. Danny didn't. And yet, he looked for the darkness just the same.

"I'll call you in a few days when I can," he said. "Just ... if you won't take off for a little while, be careful, okay? Don't go meeting any clients by yourself. Take a few days off and stay home at least. Will you do that for me?"

I should tell him about the Hawk who came to my house. I knew I should. And yet, if I had, I also knew it would make things worse. Danny couldn't help himself from coming to my rescue. I would *not* be the thing that put him in greater danger. I knew with every instinct in me that's exactly what his enemies were hoping for. I'd be damned if I'd play straight into their hands.

I heard a commotion on the other end of the phone. "I'll talk to you soon, Beth," he said. My throat ran dry. I never even got a chance to say goodbye before Danny hung up the phone. Squeezing my eyes shut, I pressed the phone to my heart.

"Please, God," I prayed. "Keep him safe. Whatever's coming, don't punish him now."

As I turned the key in the ignition, I saw Beckett Finch watching me from across the street. Of course, he couldn't hear what I'd been saying or know who was on the other end of my call. Still, the hard look in his eyes told me he knew enough.

"Well, he's settled. That's going to have to be enough for now," Darlene said. She was rummaging in the file room. After my call with Danny, I came to the office and tried to busy myself catching up on some legal research. It was fruitless really. We'd gone full stop on all active cases. Anything on the back burner would stay that way. Anything needing immediate attention had been reassigned to other lawyers. I knew they'd likely never come back. Ed had enough cash flow from his big settlement to float us for a little while, but with no new business likely to come in, things would get dire in a few months.

"Good," I said. I went to the doorway. Darlene slammed one of the big metal file cabinets shut and turned to me, dusting off her skirt.

"He's sorry," she said. "He wanted to make sure I told you that." She waddled over to the worktable we kept in here and grabbed the TV remote. This was where Darlene usually escaped to watch her soap operas when Ed drove her the most nuts. It was past eight o'clock in the evening. I should have left for home hours ago, but I didn't want Darlene to stay here alone. Sure, part of me held a little fear about going back to my house. Though I was sure I'd called my intruder's motives correctly, I was still scared.

She flipped through the channels, settling on the local news. "You should head on home, honey," she said. "Take a few days. We've taken care of everything pressing."

"Same goes for you," I said. "In fact, why don't you let me take you to dinner? I could use the company and we could both use a change of scenery."

Darlene's eyes brightened. "You know, that's not a half bad idea. Why *should* either of us sit here wallowing about Eddie or ... well ... any other man?" She shot me a conspiratorial wink then lifted the remote to turn off the TV. Something made her stop. Her mouth dropped. Instead, she turned up the volume.

"Honey," she said. "Isn't that ..."

My heart stopped cold. The news reporter stood outside a bar. The crawl across the bottom of the screen gutted me.

"That's Woody's," Darlene said. "In Port Azrael. Isn't that a biker hangout?"

I couldn't stop reading the crawl. *Gang violence erupts in Port Azrael. Two dead.*

The windows of Woody's bar were shot out and yellow crime scene tape crisscrossed in front of the door. As the reporter gave sketchy details, two men came out carrying a body bag. The ground seemed to give way beneath my feet.

Chapter 16

Deacon

Cold steel. That's what my blood felt like as I held another man's throat between my hands. I couldn't think straight. I couldn't see straight. All I could hear were the gunshots fired into the pool room at Woody's Bar.

They'd struck first. Bear had been afraid of that. Shep, Maddox, Chase, and I had gone to Woody's to warn him about the trouble brewing. We did it for all the businesses under our protection. Now it was too damn late. Woody had a bullet lodged in his shoulder. Two of his patrons were dead. Chase got grazed on the cheek. One millimeter to the left, they would have blown his damn head off.

Maddox, Shep, and I had taken off after the shooter. We'd cornered him just off Route 10. It was a Hawk, all right. Low level enough he didn't wear a patch. But his chest was covered with their ink. For now, I just called him Puke.

"Tell Bear we're going to need a clean-up crew," I said. Shep's bullet caught the puke in the arm. It went through and through. I dragged him out of his car. Maddox took care of the probie riding with him. He had him pinned to the ground, his boot on the guy's ear.

The puke's breath stank. I was pretty sure he'd shit himself. "It's your lucky day, asshole," I said as I heard the sirens pick up in the distance. Of course, one of the bartenders had called in the shots. Bloodlust coursed through my veins. I could do it. Damn every oath I'd ever taken. And every confession I'd ever made. This puke came out to spill blood tonight. Dark Saints blood. It was just our luck he was a lousy shot. But with the cops about to pull up any second, I couldn't take vengeance the way I wanted.

"Deacon, come on," Maddox said. "We've gotta bail. Let the PAPD have this one. There were at least a dozen other witnesses at the bar."

"You tell your boss," I said, putting my face in the puke's. "This won't stand. You're going to go away for a long time, kid. The Saints can get to you anywhere."

The puke was scared, but his face spread into a desperate grin. "And you tell Bear, we can get to you anywhere too. Like your girlfriend. She's got a set of sweet tits on her, Deacon. She's feisty too."

I saw red. I jerked him up by the jacket. He coughed and sputtered in my face. "What the fuck are you talking about?"

"Beth? That's her name, right? Hot little piece of ass. Crystal Falls ain't far enough away."

I don't even remember drawing back a fist. I just remember the sickening wet sound as I made contact with the asshole's jaw. Pain exploded across my knuckles. I felt a tiny bone in my hand snap. Blood spurted out of his face and he slumped to the ground.

"Gotta bail, Deacon." Shep grabbed me and pulled me off the guy. Beth. He was talking about Beth. He knew where she lived.

I stumbled backward then finally got my feet under me as the sirens drew closer. "Come on," Shep said. "Back to the clubhouse until we get further orders from Bear. There's nothing else we can do here."

"No," I said. "You go. I've got something to take care of."

Maddox was at Shep's shoulder. The two of them glared at me. "What the hell are you talking about?" Maddox said. "You need to take care of club business. No one goes off alone. Bear's orders."

"Special circumstances," I said. Maybe I should have told them everything. But at that moment, Beth was the only thing that mattered. The Hawk had said her name. He knew she was in Crystal Falls. Nothing on this earth, not even direct orders from Bear, could have kept me from going to her.

I left Maddox and Shep in the dust. I half expected them to

follow me, but they didn't. No matter what else was happening, Bear would want a status report on the shooters. I could call him later, once I knew Beth was safe.

Chapter 17

Deacon

THAT RIDE from Port Az to Crystal Falls was the longest of my life. It was well past midnight when I tore up Beth's driveway. Maybe it would have been smarter to make less of an entrance. It didn't matter. Nothing mattered until I saw her with my own eyes.

I pounded on her front door. Her motion lights came on and every dog in her neighborhood started to bark. Good. Let them. Let the world know she had a member of the Dark Saints at her doorstep that night. God help any man who tried to come between us.

Beth came to the door. It was two o'clock in the morning, but she was fully dressed in jeans and a t-shirt. Her eyes were red from crying. Without a word, she stepped back and let me in. She crumpled in my arms as I came to her.

"You're okay?" she whimpered. I said the exact same thing to her at the exact same time.

"Baby?" I showered her face with kisses, feeling up and down her arms. She was safe. She was whole. Adrenaline coursed through me. In my mind's eye, I saw Beth like I saw Sean the last time. Instead of his bloodless face laying on a coroner's slab, I saw hers. No. I would never let it happen. They'd have to kill me first.

"It was all over the news." She sniffled. "I called you a dozen times. Why didn't you answer? Oh God. I thought ..."

"Shh. Baby, I'm okay. It's okay."

She shook her head. "It's not. Don't lie to me. It's started. They shot up Woody's. Were you there? Danny, your face. Your hand. There's blood."

She pulled me into the kitchen. Grabbing a cloth, she ran it under cold water and pressed it to my bloodied hand. I couldn't feel pain. I could barely breathe.

"What happened?" she asked. I went to her kitchen table and sat down. She sank into a chair beside me and smoothed the hair away from my eyes.

"I can't talk about it," I said. "You don't need the details anyway. I just had to ... Beth. He said ..."

"They came here," she said, her voice dropping. "I should have told you but I didn't want you to fly off the handle. I didn't want you to take their bait."

My blood heated. She looked so scared, so small. I'd seen that look on her face before. Sean used to put it there. That Hawk's whispered words turned my heart to stone. I should have killed him when I had the chance.

"You have to tell me exactly what happened," I said. I didn't want to scare her, but knew she was already terrified.

She ran a hand over her face. "Two nights ago," she said. "A guy broke into the house. He was here when I came home. He didn't do anything to me. He was just here to rattle me. He wore a Hawks cut, Danny. His name was Milo. He wanted to make sure I saw it. That's why I didn't tell you. It's what he wanted."

Something broke inside of me. It felt like a waterfall. I'd kept a wall around my heart where Beth was concerned. I didn't want to hurt her. I didn't want to have to face my own guilt for the choices I made and the things I put her through. But as I took in the sight of her, pale, beautiful, whole, the wall crumbled.

"Did he hurt you?" My words didn't sound like my own. It was as if I existed outside myself, floating in some corner, watching. Then Beth touched my cheek and tethered me back to my own body.

"No," she said, her eyes glistening with tears she held back. "No, Danny. He didn't hurt me. I told you. I don't think that's why he came. He wanted to make sure I knew he was a Hawk and that I told you about it. So whatever happens, whatever you do. I'm begging you, don't play into it."

She came to me. It was as if she could brush away every

shield I'd built to protect us both with just the soft touch of her hand against my cheek.

They had been here. My enemy had put his hands on her. I knew in my heart it would break me for good if anything ever happened to this woman.

My raw need took over. I was stupid to think I could be strong or stoic where she was concerned. Beth's skin flushed with her own desire. She was just as scared as I was. Her thirst just as strong.

"Beth," I whispered.

"Shh. Don't. Don't say anything. Don't tell me the fifty reasons why this is a bad idea. I already know them all. Right now, I don't care."

I pulled her to me. We sank to the kitchen floor together in a jumble of limbs. I couldn't get her jeans down fast enough. Or mine. In the back of my mind, I wondered if I'd ever manage to get this woman to a proper bed before lust drove me mad. For now, the answer was no. I would take her on the damn kitchen tile. To hell with it all.

I was hard as steel for her. Beth wriggled out of her jeans and I tore at her thin cotton panties. I slid my hands beneath her t-shirt and found her pert nipple pebbled for me.

I needed this woman. I was starved for her. There were a million reasons why I should have just got up and walked away. But I was selfish where Beth was concerned and at that moment, no power on earth could have taken me from her.

"Deacon," she whispered. I loved my name on her lips. I was Deacon. I was Danny too, but I wanted to claim her again as I was. She arched her back and spread her legs for me.

"God," I gasped. She found me, closing her fingers around my rigid cock. She was slick and hot as I drove myself home. I planted my hands on either side of her head and hovered over her. I wanted to stay like this forever. Her slippery walls enveloped me. It was home.

Beth touched my face. Her cheeks flushed with her rising desire. She was everything. She was mine. God might damn me for being selfish. It would be worth it. God help us both.

I moved in her, loving the way she twitched around me. She was tight and warm and I knew what heaven felt like. Beth curved herself around me, hooking her ankles behind me. I slid my hands up her thighs, spreading her even wider. Then I picked up a faster rhythm. Beth gasped with pleasure. She quivered with every move I made. Tiny beads of sweat formed on her upper lip. I dug my fingers into the floor to keep traction.

I shifted my weight, pulling Beth on top of me. I wanted her to ride me. I wanted to watch her move. She pulled her t-shirt over her head and threw it against the wall. Braless, her breasts hung heavy. I reached up and kissed each nipple, rolling it gently with my tongue. I loved the little noises she made as she picked up her own rhythm, grinding against me. I wanted her to take her pleasure first. I could feel her sex throb against me.

Beth fucked me with abandon. I knew she felt what I did. She was scared. So was I. I couldn't make her promises I knew she needed. I could only offer her this. Here. Now. And she took it.

When Beth came, she threw her head back, arching her dark hair over her shoulders. I laced my fingers through hers and kept her upright. I pressed my hips into her, filling her as far as my dick would go.

"Danny!" She screamed my name as her orgasm ripped through her. She was wet and wild, gushing all around me. It drove me to the edge. I never wanted this feeling to stop. I knew in my heart it would have to last us both. Maybe forever.

As her legs quivered, I got my hands on her hips and rose off the floor. Rock hard, I stayed inside of her as I got to my feet and carried her into the bedroom. Her hair brushed my shoulders, light as a feather. I lay Beth gently on the bed.

"I want to look at you," I said, my voice thick with lust. Beth squirmed, still feeling her afterglow.

God, she was gorgeous. She trembled, parting her legs. Her nipples peaked as I ran my hands down her smooth, silky thighs. I primed myself, ready to lose myself in her all over again. She let me. Beth reached up and guided me into her. I went deep. Her juices coated me. Beth. My sweet Beth. I went up on the balls of my feet, sheathing myself to the root.

Then I took her. Claimed her. Made her mine forever. Beth clutched the sheets as I picked up the pace. I could feel her rising again. She met me thrust for thrust.

"Baby," I whispered. Then I lost myself. My seed poured out of me. Beth took it all. I came fast and hard. She cried out my name. First Danny, then Deacon. She took me. I made her mine.

Then I gathered her against me and held on tight. Beth sighed against my chest and threw one leg over my hip. We were sticky with each other. Beads of sweat poured down her temple. I wanted more. I wanted it all.

I peppered Beth with soft kisses, moving down the column of her throat. Time stopped. It had to. Because when the sun rose, I knew everything might change forever. I heard my phone ringing in my jeans in the kitchen. I knew I should answer it. It was Bear. It was the club. But for these few precious moments, I shut it all out and lived only for Beth.

Chapter 18

BETH

I FELT warm and safe in Danny's arms. As the morning sun stabbed through the curtains, I realized it had been years since I'd felt this way. Or maybe I'd never really felt this way. Sean had been a means of escape from the turmoil of my home life. Eighteen seemed like a lifetime ago. But I went from one war zone to the next.

"I love you," Danny said, turning to his hip to look at me. He brought my fingers to his lips. Warmth flared through me. I wanted him again. This man set off a firestorm inside of me. I craved him like a drug.

Reaching up, I smoothed the hair away from his brow. "I love you too."

He blinked hard, as if bracing for my words. How could he have even doubted what I'd say? "I'm sorry for this," he said.

"I'm sorry I couldn't come to you without all this ... baggage. You deserve something else. You deserve peace."

I took a deep breath. "I've had peace, I think. For the last ten years anyway. I'm not saying it's been perfect. I've kept everyone here at arm's length. Sean's demons are a hard thing to shake."

The moment I said it, I wished I could take it back. No part of Sean belonged here right now. He'd been the thing between us for far too long.

"I never told him," Danny said. "But I think he knew. I think he always knew. The trouble was, he knew the both of us way too well."

So there it was. An answer to a question I'd never let myself ask. "Danny," I said. "It was over between us. It had *been* over for a really long time. He knew it. I'd already asked him for a divorce before you and I ... ever ..."

He leaned in and quieted me with a kiss. "Sean lost any claim he had over you the first time he hit you, Beth."

I couldn't breathe. Hot tears stung my eyes. I had never come out and told Danny the details of the darkest part of my relationship with Sean. But he knew. Of course he knew.

"That doesn't absolve me from blame," he said. "But I'm done carrying the guilt of things that happened in the past. I made my choice. I can't regret any of them. The one thing I do regret is now. I came here to set you free and instead I've caught you up in another shit storm."

I ran my fingers over the hard planes of his stomach. My Danny. My Deacon. He was rough and beautiful, carved in granite. I was starting to get to know the new lines of his body, the scars, the ink. I ached for him. It came as natural as breathing. I curved my fingers gently around his cock and brought him to me. He groaned with pleasure and a wicked smile lit his face.

Our coupling had been hurried and desperate last night. Now I wanted something different. I needed him. He needed me. Danny put his hands on my hips and guided me on top of him. He was hard and ready. I was wet and throbbing for him. It shocked me how attuned my body was to his. It was as if I were built for him. Just one look or the simplest touch and he had me spinning with desire.

I took him deep, relishing how full he made me feel. I rocked slow, savoring every inch of him. Deacon's eyes flashed with lust as he watched me. He reached for me, running the pads of his thumbs over my aching nipples. Those were primed for him too. I threw my head back and sighed.

We'd put so many things between us over the years. Sadness. Guilt. Oaths we both broke. But through it all, one thing stayed sacred. It was here in the silence between us as our bodies joined. It had taken me so long to understand it, but when I was with him like this, I knew we belonged.

I came slow and hard. Danny held me up, lacing his fingers through mine. As I crested down, he pulled me to him. He kissed me once then turned me, getting me up on all fours. New heat flared through me as he entered me from behind, driving even deeper than before. He leaned forward as he came, brushing his lips against the back of my neck. His strong thrusts opened me. Then he found his release.

Later, we slept through the brightest part of the morning, feeling content in each other's arms. When I woke, the space beside the bed was empty. A little flare of panic went through me as I gathered the sheets around me and looked for him.

I found Danny in the kitchen, stirring eggs in a skillet. My heart soared. He looked up and read the expression on my face.

"I thought ..."

He smiled. "You thought I'd leave?"

I sank into one of the kitchen chairs. I'd thrown on one of the t-shirts Danny left here the other day. It hung to my knees and I loved wrapping myself in his scent. I rested my chin in my palm.

"I didn't know what to think after last night." Danny expertly flipped the eggs. He turned down the heat then slid them out of the pan onto two plates. My stomach growled as he set one in front of me and handed me a fork.

"I was going to serve you breakfast in bed."

"Mmm. It's a little late for that, isn't it?"

Danny slid into the chair opposite me. His expression darkened. My heart sank. I knew this was coming. We'd let ourselves exist in a bubble last night. But we couldn't forever.

"Do I get to ask you what happens next?" I said.

Danny reached for me. No, he was all Deacon now. He put a hand over mine. "Things might get worse before they get better. And I'm not going to sit around and let you put yourself at risk. I've done that enough."

"I'm not some eighteen-year-old girl anymore, Danny. I'm not even twenty-one. I can make my own choices."

He raised a brow. "I know that. But I won't let my choices wreck your life anymore. Nobody knows I'm here. At least, they weren't supposed to. And yet, Milo Higgins broke into your fucking house, Beth. He knows about you."

"Do you think he followed you here one of the other times you came?"

Danny sat straighter. "No. I've gone over that in my head a hundred times. But ... no. I wasn't followed."

"Well, you did draw attention. Crystal Falls is your stereotypical small town, Danny. People knew you came to see me."

His eyes narrowed. "Did someone approach you about it?"

"You mean other than Darlene and Ed? Danny, the town sheriff knows you were here. He warned me to steer clear."

Danny clenched his fist. The hard look in his eyes startled me. "Sheriff? Tell me his name."

"What, you think he's working with the Devils Hawks? Why? I mean, what could he possibly have to gain by that?"

He rose and grabbed his leather cut from the back of the chair. More than anything, I wanted to coax him back into bed with me. We were heading for something I didn't want to face.

"Beckett Finch," I said with a sigh. It would do no good to keep that little piece of intel from Danny. A quick internet search would have given him the same information.

"Finch," he said. "Yeah. I've heard of him. He's not a Crystal Falls native."

"No, I don't think so. What are you going to do?" Suddenly, that hard look in Deacon's eyes made my blood run cold. I wasn't naive. I'd trusted plenty of people in my life that I shouldn't have. And yet, every instinct in me told me I had nothing to fear from Sheriff Finch.

"I don't like this," he said. "Beth, I don't want you talking to him. I don't want you talking to anyone."

"What am I supposed to do, barricade myself in this house? It won't help. I told you, if it's the Hawks you're worried about, they already know I live here."

He pounded his fist against the counter. "You can't stay here. Beth, I need to get you someplace safe."

"And we've been over this. I'm not running again. At least ... I'm not running alone."

I hadn't planned it. The words tumbled out of my mouth without my thinking. But once I started, the desire burned through me so strong I could barely stand. "Deacon, come with me. I'll go anywhere you want, as long as you come too."

It was as if my entire life had been leading up to this one

moment. Danny and me in the middle of my kitchen. His pale blue eyes cut through me. A tiny vein throbbed in his temple as he considered my words.

I went to him, sliding my hands up his chest. "Danny, let's go. If I'm not safe here, then take me someplace else. Someplace we can *both* be safe. I don't know for sure if Finch is feeding information to the Hawks. My gut tells me he's not. But it doesn't matter. What he told me is true. You can't deny it. This club war won't end without bloodshed on both sides. It'll tear up Port Azrael. You've given enough, haven't you? Ten years. So let's go. Let's not be anywhere near it when the shit hits the fan. You told me you loved me. I've always loved you. Don't we both deserve a fresh start and a chance to be happy?"

The color drained from his face and fresh pain lit his eyes. I could see the conflict swirling behind them. For the first time in my life, there was none in me. I belonged with this man. I belonged *to* this man. But I would not stand by and watch him get hurt.

"Beth ..."

"It's simple. I know you're going to tell me you swore an oath to that club. Well, haven't you sworn one to me? You promised me ten years ago that if I trusted you, if I went away and started over, I'd be safe. Am I? Am I still safe here?"

His nostrils flared. I cut him to the quick. I hated myself a little for it, but if it meant I could protect him from himself, then it would be worth it. God help me, I went in for the kill.

"You've broken oaths before. For me. I'm asking you to do it again. For us."

He gripped my shoulders. Eyes darting over me, I watched him split in two. "Beth, you can't ask me this."

"I *am* asking. Dammit, Danny. I'm asking. I'm begging. We'll do it together. A fresh start. We'll be together. We'll go somewhere the club can't touch either of us. Don't make me lose you too. You owe me this."

He did. Even though I knew it wasn't fair of me to ask. I loved him though. And it was tearing us both apart.

"Beth, don't. You can't make me choose. These men, this club, it's who I am."

"But I loved you before all of it, Danny. You were mine."

His face fell. "I know. I'm sorry. I wish I could make things different."

"You can. We both can. Don't you see? We'll go to California. Alaska. Europe. I don't care."

He drew me to him. The solid warmth of his chest made me feel safe, even as I knew he'd break my heart.

"I cannot leave the club. Not now. I have to see this through. If I turned my back on them, I wouldn't be the man you say you love."

I tore away from him. "But you'd be alive!" Rage thundered through me. It was driven by fear but I couldn't help it. If I closed my eyes, all I could see was Danny dead.

"It wouldn't be a life I want."

"What if I asked you to choose?" I hated the choked sound my voice made. I hated everything about this.

Deacon Wade stood before me, his fists curled at his sides. A muscle in his jaw jumped. His eyes told me everything I needed to know, but he said the words anyway. "Are you?"

"I don't know."

"Because I can't. I do love you. God, I've burned for you. I will until the day I die. But I belong to the club as much as I belong to you. I thought I had a calling once, to the church. It wasn't real. It took me years to figure that out. But the club is my true calling. These men are my brothers now."

Tears flowed down my cheeks. I let out a bitter laugh. "I've had my fill of your brothers, Danny. All they ever seem to do is hurt me and tear you away."

He came to me. I let him fold me in his arms. "I'm sorry. But there *will* be an end to this."

I shook my head. "No, there won't. As long as you're a Dark Saint, it'll never truly be over. God, it was easier when you were just going to be a priest."

I don't know how long he held me like that. Forever. Not long enough. Then his cell phone vibrated in his back pocket and the world broke back in.

"I have to go," he said. "I'm sorry for this."

Sniffling, I smiled. "No, you're not. If you were sorry, you wouldn't leave."

He smiled back. It was no use. He was right about everything. There was no separating the man I loved from the patch he wore. It's who he was. I just didn't know how much of my heart I was willing to risk this time.

He kissed me one last time then walked out of my life all over again.

Chapter 19

Deacon

I COULD FEEL Beth's heart breaking as I rode away. Because mine was breaking too. She deserved better. She deserved a life where she didn't have to look over her shoulder every minute. I'd blamed my brother for hurting her and letting his world touch her. Now I'd done the same damn thing.

Milo Higgins. I would kill him when I had the chance. He'd touched Beth. He'd been in her fucking house! My fingers trembled around my handlebars and I wished I had them wrapped around Milo's skinny neck.

I don't know how fast I rode, but I made Port Az in record time. The lot was almost empty. Rufus didn't come tearing around the side. Mama Bear's car was gone too. It meant Bear had probably sent her away long term. He would have had to damn near knock her over the head to get her to go. It meant he thought shit was grave. I just hoped with the dust-up at

Woody's they'd leave Beth out of it for now. It was one of the many things I had to run by Bear.

He was waiting for me in his office. His eyes blazed with anger as I shut the door behind me.

"You answer your fucking phone, Deacon!" he yelled. "Goddammit."

I stood before him. There was no use making a single excuse. He was right to tear my head off. "I know," I said. "I'm sorry. I had to make sure Beth was okay. Some shit happened."

Bear leaned far back in his chair. The fury in his eyes hadn't lessened, but at least he didn't look like he was about to throw a punch at me. I'd take that as progress. "Well?"

"Somebody got to her," I said. "Milo Higgins paid her a visit a couple of nights ago."

"Shit," Bear said, he popped his feet off his desk. "Did he hurt her?"

"No. She didn't even tell me about it until last night. He showed up in his cut. Made damn sure she knew who he was. So Beth figured it was all about trying to scare her and stir me up."

Bear raised a brow. "Smart girl. She's probably right."

"Yeah, well, I still don't like it. How the hell does Milo Higgins or any member of the Hawks know a damn thing about Beth? How do they know where she lives?"

There was movement behind me. E.Z. let himself into the

office. Bear nodded to him and he took a seat in front of Bear's desk.

"Who else knew where she was?" I asked. "I mean, *I* didn't even know until you told me last month."

"You sure you didn't get followed?" E.Z. asked, his tone dripping with contempt.

"I'm sure," I said. "I know what I'm doing. You think I'd put her in danger intentionally?"

Bear flapped his hand. "Crystal Falls is a small-ass town. All it would take is one person to see you talking to her before the entire population knows her business."

"She said the sheriff out there, a guy named Finch, confronted her about it. She didn't seem to think he's connected to the Hawks, but who knows. I just don't like it. It needs to be dealt with. By me."

Bear and E.Z. exchanged a look. "You sure it was Higgins?" E.Z. asked.

"She read his cut. She saw his face. He killed Sean. This can't stand. Is he in custody now?"

E.Z. slammed his fist on the top of Bear's desk. "Enough. You fucking took off on Shep and Axle. You wanna answer for that?"

"I just did," I said, trying to keep my voice even. "The shooter from Woody's made it obvious someone had been to Beth's. So I went to make sure she was okay. I handled my business same as either of you would. If it was Mama, you wouldn't have waited for permission either."

"I don't need permission," Bear grumbled. "You answer to me, Deacon. You could have been walking into an ambush. Use your head."

"I can't tell you I'm sorry, Bear. It's Beth we're talking about."

"Yeah?" E.Z. turned to me. "And she's been out of your loop for a decade, Deacon. How do you know who she associates with these days?"

I laughed. "You think she and Milo cooked the whole thing up? Give me a break. She's clean, E.Z. She always has been. It's the people around her who keep dragging her down."

"Enough," Bear said. "Shit is too stirred up to be spending time on squabbling. For now, you need to get her out of town. Just to be safe."

"She won't go," I said. "Believe me, I've tried."

"Right," E.Z. said. "Why should she go if she's got protection on the other side?"

I don't remember moving, but before I knew it, I was in E.Z.'s face. "And that's twice you've nearly accused her of something she's not. I'm telling you, she is no threat to any of us. It's the other way around. Now I've paid my dues to earn her some protection. I expect the club to honor it."

Bear got between us. In his mid-fifties, he could still throw down with any one of us twenty years younger. He pushed E.Z. and me apart.

"And I said, enough. Deacon, I'm sorry, man. I don't have the manpower to spare to sit on Beth's house in Crystal Falls. We've sent half the wives to the safehouse in Abilene. Josie went kicking and screaming, but she went. She's up at the lakehouse in Corpus Christi. She took Maya and the baby. Zig's sent Gina and his kids home to her family. The DiSalvos can look after her for now. Everyone else is handling business here."

"She's a target!" I said. "And she's mine."

Bear gave me a grim nod. I knew my timing couldn't be worse. I also knew I should have never gone to see her in the first place. The whole thing had been driven by my own selfish need to see her after losing Sean. She could have heard the news about his murder from someone ... anyone else. This was my fault and we both knew it. Bear at least had the decency to keep from saying it.

"And I'll reach out to some contacts," he said. "See if I can send someone out there to sit on her place. Somebody off book. In the meantime, you don't set foot in Crystal Falls again. You don't go anywhere solo again, you hear me?"

"I can't promise you that. If she's in trouble ... if I catch an inkling that she even could be ..."

Bear put a hand up and nodded. "Not alone, Deacon. I can't afford any more of my crew going rogue."

"And this has to be answered," I said. "Where's Milo now?"

"You'd know that if you hadn't gone AWOL, now, wouldn't you?" E.Z. said.

The front door of the clubhouse opened. It would be the rest of the crew filing in to report. I should have been one of them. Bear had told me to stick with Shep. He'd trusted me to watch his son's back. I knew I'd have a reckoning with him too, but I still couldn't feel sorry. Because I was right. When Mama Bear was in trouble, Bear would move heaven and earth to get to her. And I'd left Shep with Maddox and Axle. He wasn't alone.

"They arrested Milo last night but he made bail," Bear said. "Early this morning."

My tone was cold as ice. "Then I guess we know what needs to be done."

"You need to get with Shep," he said. "He picked up the slack for you last night."

Voices rose in the outer room. One of them was Shep's. "You'll get eyes on Beth's place?" I asked under my breath so the others couldn't hear.

"He said he would, now, didn't he?" E.Z. rose. He met me nose to nose, puffing his chest out. Anger roiled through me, but I kept it in check.

I gave Bear a nod. The shit between E.Z. and me would have to wait. I left the office and headed out to the main bar. Chase and Domino were there, looking like hell. They both had wives now. The stakes were even higher. For the first time, I knew how they felt. These men mattered to me, but we all knew what we signed up for. If any of this touched the women we loved ... I couldn't even complete the thought.

"Shep with you?" I asked.

Chase and Domino exchanged a glance. It seemed I was nobody's favorite person today. I couldn't blame them. I hadn't been honest. I kept Beth a secret, thinking it would be safer for her. It hadn't mattered in the end anyway.

"Haven't seen him roll in yet," Chase said, grabbing a beer from behind the bar.

"I'm heading over to the shop," I said. "You tell him I'm out there if he comes in."

Chase tipped the neck of his bottle toward me then turned back to Dom. I left the clubhouse and headed across the yard to the body shop. I only made it halfway before a shadow dropped in front of me and an arm took me across the back.

I stumbled forward and rounded, fists raised. Shep's face was bright red with anger. Axle stood beside him, looming like a mountain.

"Where the fuck have you been?" Shep asked. He had a fresh cut above his eye.

I looked from Axle to Shep. My protective instincts still burned. I'd kept Beth a secret for so long, I wasn't sure I was ready to tell even them.

"I had something personal to take care of," I said, knowing it wouldn't satisfy either of them. It wouldn't have satisfied me if the tables were turned.

"Personal?" Axle said. "You don't get to have a personal life, Deacon. None of us do. Not now."

"Oh yeah? You gonna stand there and tell me if you thought Maya needed you, you wouldn't turn your back on every one of us for her?"

It was a low blow, but it mattered. Axle's eyes flashed. "I know how to balance both," he said. "And Maya's part of this club now. She knows the drill. Now you wanna tell me what the hell's going on with you?"

Both Shep and Axle looked at me with such vitriol, it turned my blood cold. "Are you accusing me of something?"

Axle's eyes flickered, but he stayed stone still. Shep got in my face. "I just think it's damn convenient that every time shit's about to go down lately, you disappear."

He couldn't have knocked the wind out of me any harder if he'd punched me. He might as well have.

"What the hell is going on with you two?" I asked. "Ever since Bo got back, you two and Maddox have been acting weird. And you're accusing me of something?"

"We are at fucking war," Shep said. "You have any idea what that means?"

I shoved him back. "Yeah. I do. Are you questioning my loyalty? Because you better back the fuck off. You have no idea what I've done for this club. You have no idea what I've sacrificed. I earned my way in, Shep."

It was a low blow and I didn't truly mean it. Shep was Bear's son. Bear could have played favorites, but he didn't. If anything, he was harder on Shep than any of the rest of us. But something snapped inside of me. My worry for Beth spilled over and I let it run my mouth. I instantly regretted it. When Shep cocked his fist, I didn't counter. I figured I had this coming and the truth was, I knew it would hurt and feel good all at the same time.

Shep's blow caught me square in the jaw. I staggered sideways, spitting blood. Then it was on. I lunged for him, catching him around the waist.

"Son of a bitch!" he yelled. I got my own punch off, making contact with his chin. Axle stood back. From the corner of my eye, I saw his lopsided smile.

Shep pushed me back. We ended up against the wall of the body shop. "You need to back the fuck off, man," I said. "You don't know what the hell you're talking about."

"Yeah? Then you need to clue me in."

When Shep threw another punch, I ducked. I dove at his midsection, knocking him off his feet. He landed a few more blows. So did I. We tumbled through the yard.

The crack of a shotgun blast pierced through my head. I staggered to my feet.

"Break it up!" Bear yelled, holding the shotgun toward the sky. "Son of a bitch. Sort your shit. We don't have time for this."

Axle stood beside him. "Well, Bear. I think they *are* sorting their shit."

Shep and I stood, heaving for air. Blood dripped from his nose. I had a cut in the corner of my mouth.

"You done?" Bear asked.

I looked at Shep. He looked at me. "Yeah," he answered. He held out a hand to me. I glowered at him, but took it.

"Good," Bear said. "Because I just got a call from A.J. Moss. He wants a truce. He's offering Milo Higgins for it. Get inside. We need to talk."

Chapter 20

BETH

BEING WITHOUT DANNY HURT. It physically hurt. I was afraid to turn on the news for fear I'd see some other awful salvo in the club war between the Hawks and the Saints. He told me to call him if I needed anything. At least a hundred times over the next few days I hovered my finger over his number on my phone screen. I just wanted to hear his voice. I just wanted to know he was all right. I never called. My head told me a clean break was the best for both of us. But my heart told me something else.

Ed Albright checked himself out of rehab after ten days. He walked into the office looking haggard and thin. Darlene nearly fell out of her chair. She didn't say a word to him, she just slowly rose from behind her desk, grabbed her purse and walked out the back door.

"Oh, Ed," I said. He plopped into his oversized leather office chair and stared out the window.

"I couldn't do it," he said. "Not their way. It never works, Beth. I'm better off on my own."

He'd said all of this before. I wasn't his mother. I wasn't even his sister. All I could do was slide into the chair across from him and listen.

"Will you talk to Darlene for me?" he asked, eyes pleading.

I was tired. Just ... so tired. I couldn't change Danny. I couldn't change Ed. I could only change myself. "No, I don't think I can do that, Ed. You know I love you. Both of you. But if you can't dry out and stay that way, you finally really will lose everything."

His eyes were bloodshot. He looked like he hadn't slept in days. I realized he probably saw something similar when he looked at me. "So let's talk about something else," he said. "I've heard you had some adventures of your own."

"You heard what?"

Ed's smile warmed my heart. It's not one I saw very often these days. As much as I wanted to throttle the man for getting in his own way all the time, it was hard not to love him. He'd been there for me and took a chance on me when no one else would. I'd come to him with nothing, not even a background or a single reference. He said he saw something in me and gave me a job when I couldn't even produce a driver's license yet.

"Dark Saints," he said. "You're being careful, I hope."

"Of course."

Ed nodded. "So is that biker the past you ran from? Hell, Beth, that makes you more like my sister than anything."

I smiled. "He's part of my past, yes. But he's not why I ran. And it's complicated."

"Good." He rubbed his hands together. "It's refreshing to have someone else make terrible life choices besides just me."

"Very funny. And my life is just fine." I meant it with a healthy dose of sarcasm, but the second my words landed, Ed's eyes grew heavy again.

"Oh, Beth. I'm sorry. I know I'm probably going to spend the rest of my life, such as it is, saying that to people. I know I've mucked things up pretty good. How long before the work dries up?"

I started to sugarcoat it. I rambled off a bunch of clients and dates and facts that really didn't answer the least of his questions. Ed knew it. He regarded me with those sad, keen eyes and settled back in his chair.

"How long, Beth?" he asked again.

I took a breath. "You're finished, Ed. There's nobody left. Your three biggest cases have already been reassigned. If they settle, I'll probably be able to get reimbursed for costs, but you won't earn a fee. You've got enough in savings for you to live off for a good long while. Not enough to cover payroll or your taxes for much more than a month."

"So you're out of a job. Dammit, Beth. I'm sorry. I know it's not adequate, but I am."

"I'll be all right," I said, though it rang hollow to both of us. Sure, I could probably find freelance paralegal work, but the chances of me getting something with full benefits anytime soon were slim. At least, there'd be nothing for me in Crystal Falls. My life as Beth Kennedy was over. It would be easy to blame Ed for that. Sure, he bore a large part of the blame, but this would have happened sooner or later. Maybe it didn't matter anymore.

"Can you go back?" he asked. Ed's question stunned me. One of his greatest strengths was reading people. He was downright eerie when it came to predicting how juries would behave. Now he'd trained his particular superpower straight at me.

"Go back to what?"

"I mean, are you done running? Now that your past has finally caught up with you?"

"I'll land," I said. "I always manage to. I'm honestly more worried about you and Darlene. I don't think she's going to stick by you through this one."

Ed nodded. "I already told her not to. She came to visit me at the rehab place three days ago. I bought her a one-way plane ticket to St. Petersburg, Florida. Our cousin Joy has been bugging her to move out there for two years. You know that."

Twin emotions flipped my heart: elation and sadness. Darlene deserved to live for herself. But I'd miss her. She'd been the closest thing I had to a mother pretty much my whole life.

"Maybe I should buy a ticket for you too?" he said. "Florida's as good a place to start over as any, isn't it?"

I laughed. "What, and leave all of this?"

Ed rose from his chair. He came around the desk and put a fatherly hand on my shoulder. I knew this was so hard for him. Just like Darlene, I couldn't stay mad at him. "It's time for you to go home, Beth. Wherever that is. And if it's nowhere, build a new one. I'll help you as much as I can. I do still have a few favors I haven't called in yet. You're good at what you do. Hell, you're better than me. I've got a little money saved up. I want you to have it. You've earned it."

I covered his hand with mine. "Ed, I can't take anything more from you."

"You haven't taken enough. It's been the other way around. You think I don't know how much you've covered my ass over the years? This ship would have sunk a long time ago if it weren't for you. Anything I can give you, you've earned. I won't take no for an answer."

Ed stepped back around the desk and pulled out his checkbook. I couldn't breathe. He tore off a check, folded it, and handed it to me.

"Start over, Beth," he said. "Someplace better. Now go on home. I plan on wallowing by myself for a little while."

"Ed ..."

"Don't!" He waved a hand. "I'm not gonna hit the bottle. Darlene found it all and tossed it anyway. I just need to think and I need to be alone. I'll check in with you in a couple of days. I promise."

I rose and went around the desk. I kissed Ed Albright on the forehead then did as he asked me to. I left him alone. It wasn't until I got behind the wheel of my car before I dared unfold the check he gave me. My heart dropped when I read the amount. He'd just given me fifty thousand dollars.

It was enough to start over somewhere else. Sean was dead. He couldn't hurt me anymore. I could be Beth Wade again if I wanted. I could be Beth Kennedy.

I found myself driving around Crystal Falls. It was beautiful here. Quiet. Clean. The people of this town had embraced me. Not right away, it took time. I'd found a niche here. Now that niche was slowly closing. Ed was done. This time was different. It was different for Darlene too. She'd done all she could for her brother. It was time for her to build a life of her own. And me? It had been so long since I'd even asked myself what I wanted.

I found myself driving down the quiet little street I'd called home for nearly ten years. I pulled up to the curb across from my house and put the car in park. It was mine and yet, it had always felt transient.

When I closed my eyes, I could only see Danny. My body ached for the feel of his arms around me. He was the closest thing to home I had. But could I accept him for the man he was today? This war with the Hawks would end one way or the other. There might even be peace for a while. Then what? I'd spent the first twenty-one years of my life in Port Azrael. I knew what the Saints were. Could I let myself become a part of that life for Danny?

My phone vibrated in my purse. The tone was odd. Not a call or a text. I slid it out. A big, red warning sign flashed on the home screen. It was the app Paul Sauter had installed along with the security system. It meant something had tripped the alarm.

My heart popped into my throat. Mid-afternoon, I had the curtains drawn in the front room. I looked up and down the street. There were no cars or motorcycles out here that shouldn't be. Was it a mistake?

I swiped open the app. Paul had it hooked up to three cameras inside the house. The kitchen, my bedroom, and the living room. I flipped the view from one camera to the next. The house was empty. I went back to each room, holding my breath. On the third pass, I saw it. At least, I thought I did. Just a grainy shadow, but it looked like something moved from the hallway into the master bedroom.

"Shit!"

Chapter 21

BETH

I SWIPED out of the app and called 911. The dispatcher came on right away. I hurriedly explained the situation. "My silent alarm tripped. I can see someone moving inside the house. Can you send the sheriff right away?"

I recognized the operator as Pam Bolger. We'd handled her divorce. "You just sit tight, Beth," she said. "Don't try going in that house. Someone will be there within five minutes."

She hung up. I couldn't move. Maybe the smart thing to do would have been to leave. I felt rooted to my spot. I picked up the phone again and hit Danny's number. He answered on the first ring.

"Danny," I said, breathless.

"Beth, what is it?" He knew me. God. All I had to do was say his name and he knew something was wrong. Somehow, I found the words to explain what was happening.

"It's nothing," I said. "Probably."

"No," he said, his voice grim. "You did the right thing. Don't go back in that house until I get there. I'm only about twenty minutes away. Just sit tight. Are the cops on their way?"

"I-I think so."

"Good," he said. "I'll call you when I get close. It's going to be okay, Beth." Then he clicked off. I clutched the phone to my chest as Beckett Finch's patrol car pulled up behind me, sirens and lights flashing. Behind him, another cruiser pulled up.

Beckett got out and shouted commands to the deputies under his command. Then he came to my window. I rolled it down.

"You okay?" he asked.

"Yeah. It's probably nothing. At least, I hope so."

"Well, give us a few minutes. If there's anyone in there, we'll flush them out. You stay put until I come back."

I gave Beckett a thumbs up. His deputies were already circling my house, guns drawn. I squeezed the steering wheel then pressed my forehead to it. I got my breathing under control, then two things happened at once. The powerful roar of Deacon's bike engine vibrated behind me. Then I heard the sound of breaking glass and shouts coming from the house.

I bolted upright. Deacon dismounted. He put himself in front of my window, shielding me from the house. Finch came running around the side. He stopped short when he saw Deacon standing there. Finch holstered his weapon and picked up an Alpha male swagger as he headed toward my car.

I got out. Deacon kept a hand on my arm. His eyes transmitted a warning. Let him do the talking.

"The house is clear," he said. "No sign of a break-in."

"You sure about that?" Deacon asked. He took a protective stance in front of me. My pulse thundered in my ears. I was scared, embarrassed, but mostly glad as hell to see him.

"Yeah," Beckett said, setting his jaw to the side. His two deputies came from inside the house. One of them spoke into the radio he had holstered near his shoulder.

"We're good, boss," he said to Finch. "Looks like some raccoons tipped the garbage cans over in the back."

I put a hand to my brow. "God. I'm so sorry. I feel like an idiot."

"Don't." Beckett and Deacon said it at the same time.

Beckett cleared his throat. "I'd rather come out for a hundred false alarms than for an actual dirtbag."

I couldn't help rolling my eyes. I put a steadying hand on Deacon's chest. There was way too much testosterone in this street.

"You mind telling me what the hell you're doing in Crystal Falls?" Beckett asked Deacon.

Deacon gave him a hard expression. "I was invited," he answered. "Now if you're done here, why don't you get back to writing parking tickets or whatever it is you do."

"Danny," I said. "Come on." I shot Beckett an apologetic look and practically dragged Danny toward my front door.

Beckett looked like he could kill Danny with just a glare. Danny didn't look any better. But I got him inside and bolted the door behind us.

"I'm sorry," I said. "I shouldn't have called you out here. I freaked."

Danny put his hands on my shoulders and leaned in to kiss my forehead. "It's okay, I'm glad you did. I told you too. I hate to take anything from that rent-a-cop out there, but he's right. I'd rather come out here for a false alarm."

I stepped away from Danny. His touch still burned through me. If I didn't stick to boundaries, he'd have me bent over the couch in another five seconds. God, how I wanted him to. I just couldn't go through a break-up scene with him again.

"He's not a rent-a-cop, Danny. Beckett's a former Navy SEAL, for crying out loud. And he's been a good friend."

A nerve twitched near Danny's eye. He clenched his fist. Good lord, he was jealous. I wanted to blast him for it, but that might start another scene I didn't have the strength to finish.

"Is everything okay with you?" I asked, desperate to change the subject. But no sooner had I said it, I wished I'd asked him anything else. Whatever answer he gave me would probably be a lie or a half-truth.

"What do I have to do to convince you to get the hell out of Texas for a little while?" he asked.

"It was raccoons," I said. "You heard Beckett. Raccoons and my own jumpiness. I never should have had this damn alarm system installed." I tossed my cell phone to the coffee table in my living room.

"Just for a week or two," he said.

I turned on him. "You think this shit with the Hawks will be over by then?"

He shrugged. "I hope so. You know I can't go into it. But Bear's got something in the works. Something that's going to piss half the membership off, including me. I'm glad I don't sit where he does."

I went to him. "If it means you'll stay safe, then Bear Bullock is my favorite person on the planet next to you."

It just blurted out of me. I'd spent so many of the last few days trying to keep myself together, I just wanted to fall apart in Deacon's arms for a little while. He came to me. Hooking a finger beneath my chin, he tilted my face until my eyes met his.

"I can only say I'm sorry so many times."

I reached up and tucked the hair behind his ear. "And I'm tired of the men in my life having to say it."

"I should go," he said. "But I wanna have a look around myself first."

"You don't trust the sheriff?"

His eyes burned bright with his answer. "No. Not a bit. I've already told you, I don't like you staying here. The Hawks know where you live and how you're connected to me. Your alarm system is a nice touch, but it's not going to do dick if someone really wants to hurt you."

I stood in the living room with my arms crossed as Deacon charged through my house, looking for hidden dangers. He went out the back door and rooted around in the yard, kicking aside the garbage cans. Satisfied, he came back inside.

He came to me, his eyes softer. "I think Finch was probably right. They did a shitty job picking up the garbage. The 'coons tore into it pretty good."

"I'll get it later," I said. "I'm just so tired."

"Beth, will you please let me make arrangements for you? Anywhere you wanna go. Hawaii, Europe. I can get you out of here. Just for a little while."

I went to him. "And what are the chances you'd go with me?"

He smiled. "Maybe soon. Right now I need ..."

I pressed a finger to his lips to quiet him. "Don't say it. I already know your answer."

He smiled. "And what about yours?"

I let out a heavy sigh. "Fine. You win. I'll take a vacation. You're the second person who's begged me to do that today. I don't care where. Someplace where it's not so hot."

Danny's smile warmed me from the inside out. If only he'd agree to come with me. His eyes gave me his answer though. He leaned down to kiss me. I should have pulled away. I just didn't have the strength.

Danny's kiss was soft and tender. Still, it stirred a craving in me it was getting harder and harder to deny. I reached up for him, lacing my fingers through his hair. A groan escaped from him as he fought his own cravings.

Then the world exploded in light and sound. A firecracker went off sending shards of glass flying in ten different directions. Danny went rigid in my arms, then took a staggering step backward. A red spot blossomed on his chest. He reached for me with one hand, his hip holster with the other. Then he keeled over and slumped to the ground.

Chapter 22

Deacon

I've been shot before. Once. I felt that one. The bullet grazed my shoulder and it was like a million bee stings. This time, I didn't feel anything at first. I only knew the bullet hit me by the look on Beth's face.

I dove for her, dragging her to the ground with me. Another shot whizzed by above her head. So close. Inches away. I tucked her under my body. That's when the heat in my chest turned to agony.

"Danny!" she screamed. I existed outside myself for a minute. I wasn't Danny. Danny was gone. I tried to move my arm, tried to push her further away from the danger. It felt stuck to my side in cement.

The third shot set off a bomb inside me. Adrenaline coursed through me. I found the strength to flip the table in the middle of the room and threw Beth behind it. I got to my knees and dove to the side of the room, pressing my back against the wall.

"Stay down!" I yelled. "Stay away from the windows!"

Beth's alarm system blared.

"It's the back door!" she yelled.

I spun. Movement to my left. I tried to lift my left arm to steady my aim. I had my Nine raised with my right. It was no use. Cement still encased my other arm to my side. Heat poured down my chest. In some detached part of my brain, I knew it was blood.

Beth moved. She threw something. A vase. It shattered against the far wall in a spray of glass. She didn't hit the guy, but it was enough to draw his attention for a split second. And that was all I needed. I got off one shot, hitting him right between the eyes. He staggered backward for a beat, then crumpled to the ground.

"Stay down!" I tried to yell it, but my voice came out of me in a jagged whisper. Beth didn't listen. She hurled herself toward the asshole on the ground, kicking his weapon out of his hand.

"Deacon!" She turned to me.

I belly crawled over to the shooter. He'd fallen down face first. I hadn't gotten much of a look at him before I shot him, but I didn't need to turn him over to know who it was. Milo fucking Higgins. I rolled him. Blood poured out of the hole in the back of his head. He died with his eyes open, staring in shock.

His chest vibrated and his phone rang. I flinched, my body ready for another blow. Instinct and adrenaline ruled me. I patted him down and pulled the phone out of the pocket of his leather vest. I brought it to my ear.

"Milo. Is it handled? I don't like to be kept waiting, asshole." The familiar, raspy voice on the other end of the phone cut through me with more force than Milo's bullet had. I couldn't breathe. I couldn't see straight. It couldn't be. No!

"Danny!" Beth brought me back into myself. I squeezed my hand around Milo's phone, wanting to crush it. I clicked off the call and slid it into my pocket.

Beth. I had to get to Beth.

Milo might not be alone. I wanted to shout it, but no sound would come out. My legs gave way. The last thing I remember was Beth's mouth opened in a soundless scream. Then everything went black.

Chapter 23

D<small>EACON</small>

"D<small>ANNY</small>? D<small>ANNY, WAKE UP, BABY</small>."

It was my mother's voice. She pressed a cool cloth to my head. She liked to sing to me. Silly nursery rhymes and songs she made up. I'd been playing out in the woods with Sean. We had a bet who could get to the highest branch of the tallest tree we could find. I lost. I reached for the branch above me and the one I balanced on snapped. When I landed hard on the ground, I couldn't breathe. Sean stood over me, laughing.

"Deacon!"

My mother's face morphed before my eyes. Her hair went from blonde to brown. Her eyes darkened. Then it wasn't my mother at all. It was Beth. Sweet, beautiful Beth. She was crying. I held her on a stone bench in front of the Virgin

Mary. She had bruises on her arms she tried to cover up. But I knew. I felt her pain and would have killed to end it.

"Deacon!"

My eyes snapped open. Part of me rebelled against it. It was so much more peaceful in the dark. Quiet. Warm. Light hurt. Air hurt. Soft fingers touched my cheek. It was her scent that pulled me back.

I let out a moan that tore through my chest. My left arm felt numb and in the back of my mind, I knew that was a blessing. Beth had her hand pressed against my face as I finally opened my eyes and let the full light back in.

Cold. Sterile. Harsh lights. A sickly, antiseptic smell filled my nose.

"You're in the hospital in Crystal Falls," Beth said. "You're okay. Can you talk?"

She looked like hell. Dark circles rimmed her eyes. The irises were blood red from crying. But when I looked at her, her sweet face melted into a smile.

"Hey," I said, then erupted in a round of agonizing coughs. Beth reached for a cup on the side of the bed. She brought a straw to my lips. God, the water was heaven going down.

"Are you okay?" I managed.

She smoothed the hair out of my eyes. "I'm okay. You saved my life."

"I kind of remember it as a team effort," I said.

She took a hard breath and looked back over her shoulder.

"What is it?" I said, trying to sit up. They had my left arm wrapped to my body. It ached, but there were no sharp pains. My mind felt a little fuzzy. Milo. Milo was dead. With my good arm, I went for the pocket of my vest, but it wasn't there. My shirt had been cut away. The phone. Milo's phone.

"You were lucky," Beth said. "The bullet didn't hit anything you need. Tore some muscle in your shoulder, but the doctor said it'll be good as new."

"I can ride?" I asked. Rage burned through me. The voice on the other end of that phone haunted me.

Her smile turned a little sad. "Yes. But not today, okay?"

"Is that bastard dead?"

She looked over her shoulder again. "Yes. I recognized him. Deacon, it was that Milo guy. The one who came to my house before."

Anger burned through me. That motherfucker came to kill. "Where's my stuff?" I said. Beth pointed to a plastic bag in the corner.

"The cops want to talk to you," she said. "I told them everything, but they want a statement."

"Can't do it. I need to get with my crew."

"Deacon," she said.

"What did the doc say?" I asked.

She let out an exasperated sigh. I was already pulling the oxygen tube away from my face.

"You don't need surgery," she said. "The bullet went straight through. God, there was so much blood, I thought …"

"What I need is to get the hell out of here."

"You can't! Didn't you hear anything I just said? You've been shot!"

"You said it went clean through. Didn't hit anything I might need. Beth, it's not safe for me here. And it's not safe for you if you're here with me and I don't have backup. I need to get with my crew. There's something I need to do."

She blinked hard and her face turned white. "What do you mean?"

"I know you're gonna hate me for saying this, but I need you to trust me. Milo showing up like he did wasn't a coincidence. I have to handle this."

"You think somebody tipped that Milo guy off that you were there?"

I pulled the leads out of my arm. In another minute, alarms would start going off. From what I could see of the hallway, they didn't have any cops on me at the moment. That wouldn't last.

"Yes, and I think I know who. And I'm not planning on sticking around to find out. You with me, baby?"

Beth's eyes searched my face. Two spots of color rose in her cheeks. I knew what I was asking her. In the span of a second, we were right back where we were ten years ago. She'd given everything up to get out from under Sean's baggage. Now I was asking her to take on mine.

She took a breath, then went to the wall and grabbed a tissue and two purple rubber gloves from a dispenser above a little sink.

"Hold still," she said, not missing a beat. She pressed the tissue against my arm and gently pulled out my IV. It stung, but I couldn't help but smile.

"And I'm doing this on one condition," she said.

"You name it," I answered before thinking. Knowing Beth, her condition could be a whopper.

"Whatever plan you've hatched, it better involve medical treatment at the end of it."

I leaned forward and slid my fingers behind her neck, lacing them through her hair. "It does. You can't ride with the Saints without needing a patch-up here and there."

She kissed me quick. "You call a gunshot wound a patch-up?"

"Today it is. Now we better move." I swung my legs over the side of the bed while Beth went to the curtain to act as a lookout.

"There's a clear shot to the stairs across the hall. If we're lucky we've got maybe five minutes before anybody realizes you're not here."

She had her back to me when I stood up. The room spun for an instant, but I got my feet under me. Beth gave me a hard stare when she saw my face. I didn't suppose my color was great, but I couldn't worry about it now. We needed to get the hell out of here and I needed to get in touch with Shep. He'd probably want to shoot me himself for taking off alone again, but once he understood why, I just prayed he'd be on board. And I prayed trusting him with what I knew would be the right choice.

"Come on," Beth said. She slid her arm around my waist. I hated to admit it, but I needed her for support if we were going to get out of here with any kind of speed.

Luck stayed with us. The minute we walked out of the room, another trauma pulled in in the ambulance bay. Beth moved with cat-like quickness. She shoved the door to the stairwell open and I followed her inside.

"You gonna stay upright or should I steal a wheelchair while I'm at it?" she asked.

"As long as I've got you by my side, I can handle anything."

She shot me a wink and we took the stairs. I got my feet under me again. "You got my cell?" I asked as we rounded the first flight. We had three more to go.

Beth reached into her back pocket and handed it to me. I punched in Shep's number as we took the last of the stairs. Beth did a quick check through the lobby. Her face scrunched up in worry.

"No good," she whispered. "Cops everywhere. We'll have to double back."

"This way," I said just as Shep answered. I pulled Beth by the arm and we went down one more flight, coming out near the service elevator.

"Look," I said to Shep. "I need a pick-up. I'll explain everything once I see you. Can you meet me on Route 10, Chili's diner in one hour? And Shep, tell nobody. Not even Bear."

I could hear Shep's heavy breathing on the other end. He was pissed. I just hoped I hadn't burned through all my goodwill with him. He was the second part of the plan. The first was finding a way to get the hell out of Crystal Falls without anyone seeing us.

Beth tugged on my arm. I followed her while Shep considered my question. "One hour," he said. "And whatever you have to say, it better be good." He hung up before I could even thank him.

"Come on!" Beth said. "I didn't ride in the ambulance. My car's still parked in the street."

It was risky. If the local cops were involved with the Hawks, it would make sense for them to have eyes on Beth's car. I could be leading Shep straight into an ambush. But the street was quiet. The street lamps popped on just as we got to her car. I slid into the passenger seat, feeling lightheaded again, a little giddy. If our luck held, we'd make it out alive.

Beth drove with the precision of a NASCAR driver as she lit out of town. She was careful though, keeping her speed only five over the limit until she hit the highway. Then she went like a bat out of hell.

"Where to?"

I gave her directions to Chili's. If I timed it right, we'd pull in right about the same time as Shep. All I could do was hope nobody followed us. I scanned behind us while Beth passed car after car.

The phone in her purse started to buzz. I pulled it out and my heart flared with alarm. Beckett Finch was calling. I held the screen up so she could see.

She bit her lip. "He's a friend of mine, Deacon. I know why you're worried, but I just can't believe he had anything to do with sending that thug to my house tonight. If he wanted to hurt me or you, there were plenty of other chances to do it."

"I don't know," I said. "I just know I can't trust anyone but you."

She reached for me, clasping my hand. She brought mine to her lips and kissed me. "You scared the hell out of me," she said. "I thought ..."

I kissed her back. "Never mind that. I'm okay. It's going to take a hell of a lot more than that to knock me out, Beth."

A tear fell from her eye. It was a bad joke and I instantly regretted it. "It's going to be okay," I said. "I just need to meet up with Shep. Then I'll come up with a plan to get you out of this. You'll be safe."

Beth's eyes widened. She shocked the hell out of me by slamming on the brakes and pulling over to the shoulder. A slew of cars honked and flipped her off as they whizzed by. Beth turned on me, her breath heaving with anger.

"Get me out of this? That's your grand plan? You think I want out?"

My heart thundered in my chest. Adrenaline shot through me, heightening my senses. "Beth ..."

"Don't," she said, holding up a hand. "Don't you dare give me all the reasons why I should stay away from you. Trust me, I've run through them all. Every single one, Danny. But here's the thing. I almost lost you today. For real. When you collapsed on my living room floor, I died. Do you understand? I *died*. So I don't care how crazy this all is. I don't care about your oaths and your honor or any of the rest of it. I'm not leaving you. I'm not running. Not now, not ever. If this is who you are, I don't care. I don't. I'm in love with you. Do you get that? Head-over-heels, bad-judgment love. We might both be damned to hell for it but I don't care about that either. I want to be with you. I belong with you. No matter what. If you want to be a priest, I don't care. If that cut is who you are, I don't care. As long as I ..."

I stopped her with a kiss. God help us both, I was starved for her. It was crazy, just like she said. I could run through all the rational reasons why making her go made sense. This was dangerous. Reckless. But as Beth melted against me, the only thing that mattered was my love for her.

She was sobbing fat tears when I pulled away. "I love you," I whispered. "Are you sure?"

She nodded, hiccupping. "Yes. Danny ... Deacon ... yes. I love you. I want to be with you. You're my heart. I bloody well won't live without you. Do you hear me?"

I went rigid. Beth's eyes widened and she touched my face. "What is it? Danny? Are you hurt? Tell me!"

A smile split my face as I pulled her against me again. "It's just ... thank God." Then I kissed her long and hard.

Chapter 24

DEACON

THERE WERE fifteen million reasons why I should have turned Beth away. She was better off without me. Safer. She could have gone anywhere. Lived any life she wanted. But when she looked at me with those steely eyes and opened her heart, I knew my own would never fully beat again unless she was with me.

When we came up for air, two more car horns blared as they passed. She'd parked at a crooked angle on the shoulder.

"Come on," I said. "It's not safe to stop this long."

Nodding, Beth put the car in gear and carefully pulled back into traffic. I wanted to touch her. I wanted to hold her hand, kiss her, pull her against me. Her presence fueled me. Later, I knew I'd crashed. When Mama Bear got a hold of me, she'd probably half try to kill me herself for leaving the hospital.

Beth might even help her. For now, with Beth by my side, I felt invincible.

I pointed the way and Beth quietly pulled into Chili's diner, picking a parking spot beneath a broken light. We could stay better hidden that way.

"Come on," I said. "We're better off inside. When Shep gets here, do you mind waiting in one of the booths? I've got some things to say to him. He won't talk in front of you. Not yet."

Beth nodded. "Fine. But I'm staying close. You still look half ready to topple over. I see so much as a cough out of you, I'm calling for an ambulance."

I gave her a salute then hooked my hand through hers as we made our way into the little highway diner.

We drew some open-mouthed stares as we walked in. It was the last thing I wanted. I had bloodstains on my shirt. I covered what I could with my leather jacket, but we stuck out. The sooner I could get Beth to the safety of the clubhouse, the better.

I didn't have to wait long before Shep walked in. He wasn't alone. He brought Axle, Bo, and Maddox with him. They spotted me right away. God, I hoped I was placing my trust in the right people with what I had to say. I leaned over to Beth. She'd taken a seat at the counter.

"Wait here," I said. "I'll call you over." I rubbed her arm with my thumb. I had a lot of explaining to do. Beth was just part of it.

Shep looked grim. He gestured with his chin and met me at an oversized booth in the back. Axle and Maddox took the seat facing the front door. Bo slid in, then me. Shep took the last space, caging me in between them.

"What the fuck happened to you?" Axle asked.

Now that I had them here, I didn't know where to start. So I cut to the end. "I've been seeing Beth. She was Sean's wife. I came out here to tell her what happened to him and then ..."

Axle put a hand up. "I get it. And I remember. She was special to you. But why the hell didn't you tell us that before?"

"She's been through enough. Sean's shit ... I tried to keep her clear of mine."

Shep pulled on my jacket. "Looks like you failed. What happened?"

I filled them in as best I could. I told them everything, how Milo first threatened her, my suspicions about the local Crystal Falls cops, then the shitstorm at her house. Finally, I pulled Milo's bloodied phone out of my jacket and lay it on the table between us.

"Milo's dead," I said. "I killed him. But he got a call. I answered it. I never said a word but the caller on the other end ... I recognized his voice."

Three words I had left to say. The moment I did, it would change everything. I had nothing left to go on but my gut. I put my trust in these four men.

"It was E.Z.," I said.

Shep sat upright, but his face didn't register shock. Instead, he gave a grim look to Axle.

"You're sure?" Bo asked.

Nodding, I tapped the phone. "He probably called on a burner, but it'll be the last call. He was asking Milo if he handled something for him. I believe it was me. I think E.Z. wanted me and Beth dead."

"E.Z. knew where Beth was living all this time?" Shep asked. He was staring straight at Axle when he asked.

I scratched my chin. From the corner of my eye, I saw Beth staring. She tried to look away when I caught her eye, but it was too late. I made a gesture to her. *Just sit tight, baby.*

"Bear and E.Z.," I said. "It was the deal I made. Ten years ago, when Sean first started dealing for the cartel, they leaned on him. He was into them for a ton of money. I don't know how he ended up working out, but there were casualties along the way. They came to Sean's place looking for Beth. They were going to kill her to keep him in line. Only she wasn't there that night. She was with me. My dad was there instead so they killed him."

"Shit," Axle said. "I always thought it was something like that."

"So you went to Bear," Bo said.

I nodded. "I needed to get protection for Beth and the rest of my family. And revenge. Bear made the arrangements, but I carried it out. I took out the hitman who killed my dad. Bear wanted him gone anyway. There was some club shit brewing that didn't involve me, but it was a two-birds-with-one-stone deal for him. I left the priesthood. I had no choice. It wasn't for me anymore after what I'd done ... what I'd seen. I patched in not long after that. Bear promised Beth a new identity and a new life. I made him swear never to tell me where she was. I thought it would be easier ... better for her that way. I was stupid enough to think it should be part of my penance. Then Sean died and ..."

"And you love her," Maddox said. He, Bo, and Axle had found women of their own. I never envied them before. Now I understood. My eyes caught Beth's again. Her soft smile melted me.

"You're sure nobody but Bear and E.Z. knew where Beth was?" Bo asked. "And you're *sure* it was E.Z.'s voice you heard on Milo's phone?"

"I'm sure. And none of you seem surprised."

Shep cleared his throat. "We're not."

My heart thundered in my chest. I took a sip of water the waitress had set out for us. "Then you better tell me what the hell's going on."

Axle answered for them. "We've been working with a guy on the inside," he started. "One of the Hawks approached us a few months ago. Said he had reason to think somebody in the club was working against us."

"A rat within *our* crew?" I asked; my heart dropped. I knew the answer now. Still, I had to keep saying the words so I could believe it. E.Z. He'd been working against us all along.

"I didn't want to believe it either," Bo said. "But there's been a bunch of other shit. Shit I couldn't talk about. It's the reason I had to stay away for so long."

"This club war," Shep said. "My pops never wanted it. He got backed into a corner. I don't think the Hawks' prez wanted it either. Too many things haven't added up. Now with this ... I think we have our answer."

Axle let out a heavy breath and squeezed his eyes shut. When he opened them, he'd gone stone cold.

"Bear's been trying to negotiate a truce," Shep said. "I think E.Z. knew if Milo took out one of us, there'd be no way for that to happen. He knew you'd tear off to Crystal Falls alone. You were the perfect target. Plus, Milo was the bait my pops wanted to dangle. We already had him fingered for killing Sean. If the Hawks' prez had been willing to give him up, Bear might have been able to use that."

"And I killed him," I said. "It was a win-win for E.Z. If Milo had killed me and Beth, there'd be no way Bear could broker peace. The rest of the club would never go for it. And now, I've killed Milo ... the Hawks won't take that lying down."

"E.Z. knew exactly what he was doing," Axle said.

"So what do we do now?" I asked. "Do we take this to Bear?"

Again, those secret looks passed among them. Axle leaned forward. "Not yet. If we know anything, it's that E.Z.'s played this smart. He's been one step ahead and planned for every contingency. Like tonight. No matter how it shook down, it would have ended up in his favor. He wants war. As much as it kills me, we have to bide our time. We have to figure out what that fucker is planning. Cuz if I know one thing, it's that he's got a backup plan to his backup plan."

"So we do nothing? We sit tight?" I asked.

Shep nodded. "For now. Yes. We protect our own. We figure out a way to bring E.Z. down from the inside out. When the time is right, we'll bring it to my pops. We still don't know if E.Z. is acting alone."

"You think Bear's in on this?" I asked, my heart nearly flipping inside out.

Shep's expression was grave. It told me all I needed to know. I couldn't believe Bear could be working with E.Z. I wouldn't believe it. But Shep and the others were right. Until we figured out E.Z.'s end game, our best weapon against him was secrecy. We'd have to find a way to beat him at his own game. And we would. I knew it in my heart.

Beth came to the table. "He needs a doctor," she said. "Either you boys wrap this up or I'm calling 911."

Axle's face split into a smile. He leaned over and held out his hand to Beth's to shake. She glowered at him, but took his hand. I could tell by the flicker in Axle's eye that he respected her grip.

"I've got to ask you something, Beth," I said. "After all these years, when you left Port Azrael, who was your contact with the Saints."

"It was always Zeke Watson," she said. "He drove me to Crystal Falls that first night. He gave me a number and told me if shit ever hit the fan, I should call him. I never did though."

Bo dropped his head. He pressed the bridge of his nose between his thumb and forefinger. My stomach flipped and it got hard to breathe.

"Enough," Beth said. "I mean it. Whatever you have to talk about, it can wait. Deacon needs to get to a doctor."

"I'm fine," I said holding up a hand. "We'll have Mama Bear check me out. If she wants me back in the hospital, it'll be in Port Az."

"He's right," Shep said, rising. "We can keep Deacon safer in our own backyard. Let me make a couple of calls. I'll find someplace safe for you, Beth. Don't worry."

She looped an arm around my waist. I pulled her close. "I'm not worried," she said. "And I don't leave Deacon's side."

Shep, Axle, Bo, and Maddox exchanged looks. "Like that, is it?" Axle smiled.

"Yes," Beth said, her tone taking a hard edge.

Maddox covered his mouth to hold back a laugh. "Perfect," Bo said. "Looks like you're going to fit right in. Congratulations, Deacon, though this means Dom wins the pool."

"The pool?" I asked.

Shep slapped me on the back. "Chase thought you were probably heading back to the seminary," he said. "Ever since you started disappearing. A few of the guys, Dom mostly, figured it was a woman. The rest of us …"

His voice trailed off. "Shit," I said. "You thought it was me? That I turned traitor?"

Axle squared his shoulders and stared at me head on. "It doesn't matter what anybody thought. It only matters what is and we know what we need to do. Now come on. Beth's right. You look like shit. We brought the van. Bo's driving. Shep and I will ride beside you. Honey, you okay with ditching your car? It's better that way if anyone put a tail on you. You won't need it. The club will take care of you from now on. That is, if you're with Deacon."

Beth squeezed her arm tight around me. She straightened her back and looked at Axle dead in the eyes. There weren't many people ballsy enough to do that and live to tell about it. But my girl was made of steel.

"I'm with Deacon," she said, lifting her chin.

Axle smiled. "Well then, that's good enough for us. Let's get the hell out of here and go back home." With Beth by my side, the word took on greater meaning.

Her stride was sure and strong as I led her to the back of the club van. I climbed in and held my hand out for her. Smiling, she stepped up and slid right back into my arms.

"You sure about this?" I asked. "Life as my old lady might get pretty bumpy."

She laughed. Her soft hair tickled my chin as she slid beneath my arm in the space where she fit best. "Bumpier than today?"

I kissed her. "Let's hope this is the high-water mark, but maybe."

"I don't care," she whispered. "I know I should, but I don't. I've wasted too many years living for other people or just waiting to live at all. I want this. I want you. I don't care where it takes us as long as it's together. Do you think you can live with that?"

My heart soared as we hit the highway at top speed again. Bo drove smooth, but I still winced every time we took a curve. It earned me a stern look from Beth. I knew Mama Bear would have my ass next.

"Yeah." I smiled as Bo made the turn for the Port Azrael bridge. Its LED lights blazed a rainbow of colors across the night sky.

"It's so pretty." Beth gasped, looking out the window. "I've stayed away. Did you know that? I haven't been back here. Not once. Now I can't imagine being anywhere else."

I leaned against the back of the van. Beth snuggled against me, careful not to put her weight on the wound on my shoulder. I supposed it should hurt like hell. With her in my arms, I felt invincible.

"I love you," I said. "I think you're crazy as hell to want to stay with me, but I'm done trying to drive you away."

"Good." She laughed. "Because you can't."

It wouldn't be easy. This club war was far from over. Ousting E.Z. might tear us apart. But for now, as Beth pressed her cheek against me, the bridge lights brightened. Port Azrael spread before us. For the first time in my life, with Beth in my arms, I felt like I was truly going home.

Chapter 25

BETH

TWO MONTHS LATER ...

"THERE," Josie "Mama" Bullock said. She'd just finished adjusting a string of pearls around my neck. They were hers. My something borrowed. She pressed her cheek to mine, catching my eyes in the mirror.

She was a striking woman with silvery-white hair cropped short. She was strong, smart, fiery. I loved her almost the minute I met her at the same time she scared the hell out of me. But she loved Deacon. She'd given him a family after his own had fallen apart. For that alone, she'd have my eternal gratitude. She gave me something else along with it: her friendship.

"Thank you," I said, my eyes misting. She scolded me about my makeup for about the sixth time. I stood up, smoothing my white silk dress. It was just a simple sheath with spaghetti straps. I didn't want ruffles or anything flashy. I'd done all of that before.

"He loves you so much," Mama Bear said. "And you brought him back to me."

"Funny," I said. "I was just about to tell you the same thing. You kept him whole all these years."

She shrugged. "Oh, I don't know about that. I think that boy was broken into pieces until he found you again. I never knew you were the thing missing. If I had, don't think I wouldn't have dragged you back here years ago. The hell with what Deacon had to say about it. You two belong together. You've suffered enough apart."

She reached for me, pinning a stubborn strand of hair back into the French knot she'd helped me make. I slid into my satin heels and stepped back.

"You're perfect," she said.

There was a soft knock at the door. Deacon stepped in. Mama gave him a wry smile then excused herself quietly.

"It's bad luck for you to see me!" I gasped even as my heart fluttered with excitement.

Deacon came to me. God, he was so handsome. He'd tied his hair back. His blue eyes shimmered. He wore a sleek, black suit. I reached up to straighten his tie. Somehow, he managed to look just as dangerous as he did wearing leather.

Deacon slid his hands around my waist and pulled me to

him. "I couldn't wait. I needed to make sure you were still real."

I went up on my tiptoes and kissed him. "I'm real, baby." I gasped as he got his hands beneath my ass and lifted me off my feet. He took three steps forward and set me on the vanity table. This was the cry room of San Mateo's church. The place doubled as a staging area for the bridal party on wedding days. I had no party. Mama Bear would stand up for me. Bear would be there for Deacon. It was all we needed and perfect to seal our vows to one another.

"I want you," Deacon whispered.

"What, now? We're just about to go out there!"

"Yeah." His voice rippled along my neck as he kissed a trail up it. My nipples peaked and heat coursed through me. Oh. I wanted him too. It nearly drove all reason out of my head.

I growled with pleasure. "Danny, it's probably a sin. We're in a church."

He laughed. "I've done worse. And if this sends me to hell, baby, it'll be worth every second."

I threw my head back and joined his laughter. Deacon found the hem of my dress and slid his hands between my legs. Afraid of panty lines, I hadn't worn any underwear. It seemed like a good idea at the time. Now it drove me mad with lust.

Deacon nipped my ear and pried my thighs apart. Gasping, I braced myself against the counter as his skilled fingers found the slippery cleft between my legs. He hooked three fingers together and slid them into me.

"Oh," I gasped. "Baby."

"I want to hear you say it," he said.

"Yes. Oh God. Yes. Do it. I can't wait anymore either."

I tugged at Deacon's fly. I got it open and found him huge and hard. I hiked my dress up all the way. Damn the wrinkles. Deacon entered me in one powerful thrust.

"You're mine," he whispered as he started to fuck me. I was drunk with desire. Part of me didn't care who heard. I knew Mama Bear would be discreet and drive the others away. God bless that woman for so many reasons.

Deacon felt so hard, so good. I opened for him like a flower. I'd been so wet, so ready for him, it didn't take long before the rising tide of my desire carried me away. I bit into his shoulder to keep from crying out with the ecstasy of it. Deacon held still inside me, letting me find the sweet friction that would drive me home.

As I crested down, he slid out of me. I surprised him that day with a gift of my own. Smiling, I went down to my knees and took him in my mouth.

"Baby," he gasped. As quickly as I found my pleasure, Deacon was no match for my lips and tongue. I took him. All of him. He gripped the side of the counter and I brought him home.

He helped me to my feet and kissed me deep. "I love you," he said.

Laughing, I reached down to gently zip his fly. "I love you too. But you're a bad influence," I whispered.

There was a light knock at the door. "Danny, we're ready for you." It was Father Sanchez. Though it had been hard won, he gave us his blessing when Deacon brought me home. He worried about both of us, but I knew the priest wanted Deacon to be happy. He had been there for me too when my life fell apart. Having him marry us today felt like coming full circle. Ten years ago, Deacon was meant to take one oath with Father Sanchez. Today, he would take another with me.

Giggling, I straightened Deacon's tie as he smoothed my hair for me. "Well, you'll have some interesting things to talk about in the confessional."

Deacon kissed me and lightly slapped my ass. "No way, baby. I'm not the least bit sorry for this one. Come on. Time to make you my wife."

I gave him a salute. "All yours, husband." It was good and right. My eyes filled with tears of joy again as I looked at my handsome groom.

Deacon's face grew serious. I knew what was on his mind. Our day would be filled with hope and laughter. But there was something else beneath all of that. He wouldn't tell me everything, but I knew enough.

With Milo Higgins's death, the clubs had reached a temporary truce. Milo killed Sean and tried to kill Deacon. He'd paid with his life. But Deacon feared that wouldn't be the end of it. He wouldn't say more. As the almost wife of a Dark

Saint, I learned quickly there were things he'd keep from me. I was okay with that. Because I had the part of him that mattered most. I had his heart. In a few more minutes, I would have his name. It was enough. It was everything.

Deacon gave me my life back. He told me I gave him his soul. Maybe I had, but I still felt like I got the greater part of the bargain. I had something else as well. With the money Ed Albright gave me, I had another dream to fulfill. This fall I was starting law school. I had my life back. I had my heart.

As we walked out of the cry room and stood at the end of the aisle, my heart nearly burst with joy. Deacon's brothers stood. I'd gotten to know them all over the last months. They embraced me, treated me like a sister. In time, I knew I would grow to love each of them. I would worry for each one of them in the coming weeks and months. Though the clubs had reached a break in the tensions, we all knew it wouldn't hold. War still loomed over Port Azrael. But I would not run from it. I would never run again.

Deacon and I locked hands. He smiled down at me as we walked down the aisle together. My man. My love. With Deacon at my side, I knew whatever came, we could face it with strength and hope. And I knew where I belonged.

THE END

ALSO BY JAYNE BLUE

Dark Saints M.C. Series

Dark Vow

Dark Temptation

Dark Honor

Dark Fury

Dark Desire

Dark Instinct

Dark Seduction

Dark Destiny

Dark Oath

Dark Redemption

Great Wolves M.C. Series

(Biker Romance)

Dex

Sly

Colt

Kellan

Sawyer

Brax

Stone

Ryder

Nash

King

Tortured Heroes Series

(Men in Uniform Romance)

Vice

Heat

Marked

Strike

Ripper

Edge

Uncaged Series

(MMA Romance)

Ride

Clinched

Stripped

Hooked

Hold Series

(MMA Romance)

Book 1

Book 2

Book 3

Hold Series Box Set

Torrid Series

(Billionaire Romance)

Book 1

Book 2

Book 3

Complete Series Box Set

The Owned Series

(Billionaire Erotic Romance)

Owned by the Playboy

Owned by the Candidate

Owned by the Spy

Owned by the Prince

Owned by the G-Man

Complete Series Box Set

Made in the USA
Columbia, SC
24 November 2021